A WELCOME AT CLOUD COTTAGE

ZARA THORNE

BLOODHOUND BOOKS

Print ISBN: 978-1-917705-09-7

CHAPTER 1

What is this place? What am I doing here?

Tilly hesitates. Her head – her feet, too – suddenly all of a dither. She sees shapes all around her, and colours. So many colours. And lights, shining down from above, burning holes in her skull.

Somebody brushes past her, bumping her arm. She's in the way but she can't move, not until she knows... Right, this is a shop. She walked here from home, just now. Of course she did. It's the village shop. She's got it now. Its old name flashes up like neon before her eyes: Raymond's General Stores, except they don't call it that any more. Something else. The new name refuses to come.

It doesn't matter. Tilly gives herself a mental shake. Her head thumps. Somehow, her feet move and she continues her perusal of the shelves.

Cereals. Here they are. Have they moved them again? Or have they been there all along? She can't see the one she wants. The one in the blue box with some sort of animal on the front, the one that should have come on the van with the rest of the shopping, but didn't. The man brought cereal but it was the wrong sort. And he didn't bring any butter at all! Seems they were out of stock. Fancy a big place like that running out of basics. Always best to go and get these things yourself.

But the man with the van is so convenient. Except when he hasn't brought any butter and he's come with the wrong cereal. Not the kind... she – the name escapes Tilly – likes best. The one in the blue box.

She reaches up to the top shelf. The movement makes her dizzy for a moment. Her hand wanders along the row of cereal boxes, detached, indecisive, as if it has a mind of its own but has temporarily mislaid it.

Or Tilly has. One or t'other.

That doesn't make sense for a start, Tilly thinks. Not much does this morning.

She stares at the box of cereal that's found its way into her wire basket. It seems familiar. If it's wrong, she'll just have come back tomorrow for the right one. Not the end of the world. The curly writing on the box won't keep still. The picture of the animal buckles and slopes, as if the creature is about to leap right off the box.

And then she loses her grip on the basket as something hits her, hard, on the back of her head. Or that's what it feels like. The shapes and colours have all changed places. Up when they should be down. Down when they should be up. How curious, Tilly thinks.

Whose feet are those, sticking up in front of her where they've no business to be?

She blinks, tries to focus. She makes out a face, then more faces, hovering over her. Pale, like moons. She can hear voices falling over each other. Hollow and distant, as if they're coming from inside a tunnel.

'Poor old thing. Collapsed, just like that!'

'Went down like a bag of spuds.'

'She didn't look right when she came in. She looked grey in the face and a bit confused, I thought.'

'I said that, didn't I? Didn't I say that?'

'What happened, love?'

'Don't worry. Stay where you are.'

'Don't move. That's it, now.'

Something soft is pushed under Tilly's head. The faces don't look like moons any more. They're a mass of black dots.

Tilly hears but she can't see. *How odd.*

A tinkling sound. The shop door? More voices, too far away to make out what they're saying.

A woman's voice, firm, calm, rising above the others.

'Don't let anyone else in, not till we've dealt with this.'

'I've got to get home.'

Was that Tilly's own voice? She tries to raise itself upright but her body's not co-operating.

Someone's bending close. 'What's your name, dear? Does anyone know who she is?'

A man speaks. 'It's Mrs Donnelly. Matilda Donnelly. Not seen her down here in a while.'

Donnelly? Who's that?

'I've got to get home.'

'Not for the minute, love. Let's get you sorted first.' A hand, gentle, cool, stroking her forehead. 'Is there someone we can call? Someone who can come and fetch you?'

'Lives on her own, doesn't she? Widowed, years back.' The man again. 'There was a youngster at one time, granddaughter, niece or summat, used to live with her. Mind you, that was ages ago. She won't be there now.'

'Oh, she won't still be there! That was ages ago.'

'That's what I just said!'

What's she doing down here? Something's gone wrong, Tilly thinks. Although she can't seem to work out what it is. Her fingers pluck at the material of her skirt. She needs to get home but nobody's listening.

The shop door pings again. Black shapes, figures, emerge through the dots, fussing around her. *Busy, busy.*

'That's it now. Up we come.'

Tilly senses herself being hoisted up, then her back finds a resting place.

'Are you taking me home?' she asks.

Or perhaps she doesn't. The words might just be in her head, which is spinning like a fairground carousel.

Either way, nobody answers.

CHAPTER 2

Ramona Donnelly jumped down from the bus, landing lightly on the narrow strip of weed-strewn grass bordering the tarmac. The driver gave a merry double toot on the horn as the bus moved off with a belch of diesel, carrying the few remaining passengers along the lanes and down into Charnley Acre. Ramona was usually the only one to get off the bus at this stop on the outskirts of the village, where houses were few and there was nothing much around except fields and trees.

Her phone buzzed in her pocket as she walked along the verge, keeping close to the hedge in case of passing traffic. She took out her phone and smiled when she saw Lilah's name and her madly waving avatar. What could there be left to say? They'd only parted company half an hour ago. Lilah had waited at the bus stop with her before the short walk to where she lived, in a village ten times the size of Charnley Acre.

But there was always more to say.

See you tomorrow. Ramona read, noting the absence of a question mark.

Tomorrow was Saturday. They sometimes met up on a

Saturday and caught a bus to Lewes or Cliffhaven to wander round the shops. They never bought much – the shops in Lewes were limited and expensive, and Cliffhaven wasn't much better – but it was somewhere to go and both places had good cafes to hang out in. Cliffhaven had the beach, too; handy if the weather was good.

Ramona thought for a moment. While she was thinking, a second message pinged through.

Oh go on. Say yes.

She stood still and texted back. *Might do. Let u know in morning.*

She wasn't sure yet what she wanted to do tomorrow. Besides, her grandmother might need her to help with something. Not that she ever stopped Ramona from going out and seeing her friends. She'd never do that, which made it all the more important that she didn't spend all her free time away from the cottage.

Continuing along the roadside – the verge had run out now – Ramona passed the entrance to the farm, then the gate opening onto the path that wound its way up to the South Downs, and, finally, the apologetic scattering of cottages that looked like they'd been dropped there by accident.

A minute later, she reached the turning to home. Grassy underfoot, treacherously muddy in wet weather, the turning looked as if it led nowhere, unless you knew. Trees and bushes grew on either side, partially concealing a partly broken-down fence. A sharp left turn and there was the cottage, hidden from the road by the trees. The best view of it was from high up, on top of the Downs. White painted with a grey slate roof, from up there it looked like a doll's house that somebody had forgotten and left in the corner of the field.

The cottage had a long back garden, and a narrow strip of garden at the front. There was no path or gate. A weathered sign attached to a tree on the left-hand side was faintly inscribed with the words: *Number One The Pasture*. Ramona had long since given up wondering why it had been necessary to call it Number One when there was no number two, or three.

Shifting her rucksack from her back, letting it dangle in one hand, Ramona walked round to the back door and turned the brass knob. The door didn't budge. It was never locked unless they were both out. Funny that it was locked now, Ramona thought. She had a key to the front door but she was here now. She lifted the large, flat stone that lay beside the wall and groped beneath it for the spare key to the back door. A moment later, she stepped into the kitchen, shutting the door behind her.

'Tilly? It's me!' As if it would be anyone else.

There was no answer. The wing-backed chair in the corner of the kitchen was empty, Tilly's library book on the floor next to it, the leather bookmark poking out like a tongue. Perhaps her grandmother was 'out back', as she called it; 'out back' being the small bathroom converted long ago from the old outside toilet and scullery.

Ramona went back through the kitchen and tapped on the bathroom door.

'You in there, Tilly?'

Silence, except for the insistent warble of a wood pigeon from the trees at the back of the cottage.

Frowning, Ramona went through the hall and up the creaky, twisting staircase to double check, but Tilly wasn't in her bedroom, which meant she was definitely out. The locked back door had been a sign, of course.

Crossing the landing to her own bedroom, Ramona changed out of her school uniform and into jeans and a grey hoodie. Back downstairs, she made a jam sandwich, and sat in the living room to watch TV. Homework could wait. She had the whole weekend to do that.

One programme ended and another began. Ramona's mind wandered across the possibilities. Tilly was hardly ever out at this time of day. She belonged to the old-fashioned school of ideas which said that a child – even a twelve-year-old like Ramona – shouldn't come home to an empty house. If she did have to go out for any reason and she'd not said beforehand, she always left a note. But not this time. It was a *bit* funny, Ramona conceded, but nothing to worry about.

Ramona wasn't a worrier by nature; she preferred to apply logical thinking to whatever the current situation was. Logic was one of her strong points; a teacher had once said that to her. Ramona was inclined to agree.

But time drifted on and Tilly didn't come home. There weren't even any signs in the kitchen that dinner had been prepared earlier. She was actually quite hungry, as Tilly must be by now. Maybe she should do something about dinner herself. That would be the grown-up, responsible thing to do. But she wasn't that confident with cooking, and she didn't know what they were having anyway.

She went to the front door, opened it and looked about. And then, when there were no signs of movement, she went out and into the field for a proper look. The field was quiet and empty, as always. There were clumps of trees on its edges. She checked each clump, rustling around among the woody bits and tall grass without knowing what she was looking for, or hoped to find. She even walked all the way up the sloping field and peered inside the tumbledown shepherd's hut. Tilly wasn't there, of course. Ramona didn't think she would be.

She screwed up her forehead to help the thinking along. She'd already counted the buses which passed the door, not only by the faint rumbling but by the times they went past. If Tilly had gone to Cliffhaven or Lewes to do a bit of shopping, which she sometimes did, she might have missed one bus back but not three.

Tilly had a friend who lived on the fringes of Lewes, in a big modern house that was always full of children of various ages. The friend's name was Mary Something. She was a very small person, slim, with bright eyes that followed you everywhere, like a little bird. She wasn't as old as Tilly; at least, she didn't look like she was. The children weren't Mary's; Ramona had never asked whose they were. Mary had a husband called Richard, who had a smiley red face and a Father Christmas beard, only it was brown, not white. Ramona had been to the house with Tilly lots of times when she was younger, and had played with the children. They had a big garden, with swings and a slide, as well as bikes and scooters everyone shared. She didn't so much now because she was usually at school, and she'd grown out of kids' games yonks ago. The last time she'd gone with Tilly to visit Mary had been in the Easter holidays, she thought. She'd sat around, feeling bored while the women talked.

Mary was Tilly's best friend, the same as Lilah was Ramona's. Best friends could never have enough of each other's company. If her grandmother had gone to Mary's, she might have missed several buses. They could talk for England, those two.

So, Tilly must have gone to see Mary and had lost track of time. It was the only logical explanation. She might not have been bothered about hurrying home, accepting that Ramona was perfectly capable of looking after herself. The idea sounded plausible, and made her feel more positive, even cheerful. But even if she was at Mary's, it wasn't like Tilly to be out this long without leaving a note or a message. Not like her at all.

Ramona tried to focus her mind on other possibilities. She could only come up with one: Tilly might have gone to the medical centre to see the doctor. She'd could have made an appointment and forgotten to tell Ramona about it this morning, before she went to school – that could be it.

Tilly had been a bit forgetful lately; Ramona had noticed that. It wasn't usually about anything important, like dates and times, but silly things like leaving the washing liquid out of the machine so the clothes were washed in plain water, or standing the empty plastic milk bottles outside the door because she'd forgotten the milkman stopped delivering glass ones in, like, 1980 or something. They'd had a good laugh about that, the two of them. That was after Ramona had found the bottles outside, all nicely washed out, and had held one up in front of Tilly, with a clearing of her throat and a question in her eyes.

'Oh, how stupid! What am I like?' Tilly had snatched the bottle, picked up the others and flipped them inside the recycling bin. 'I should audition for *Doctor Who*. I'd be good at the timeslips!'

'You would,' Ramona had said, wildly imagining her grandmother going into the Tardis. 'It might just be the hot weather that's made you forget the milk thing,' she'd added, feeling a tiny bit more serious than she had before. It hadn't been hot at all, quite chilly, really.

But Tilly was kind of old; she was bound to forget the odd thing. So, perhaps today she'd simply forgotten about the doctor's appointment, the receptionist had rung to remind her, and she'd gone rushing down to the village in a sweat.

Ramona looked at the clock. The medical centre closed two hours ago.

CHAPTER 3

The thing was – Ramona emptied a tin of baked beans into a saucepan – the thing *was*, of all the people in the world, Tilly was the one she could trust completely. No chance of failure. In which case, a little thing like Tilly being late home – okay, *very* late home – might be a ripple in the day, something to be talked about later to make sure it never happened again, but that was all it was. A ripple in the day. Or a blip. Yes, that was a better word. A Tilly sort of word.

Before she'd made a start on her tea, she'd sifted through the random collection of items in the brass letter rack in the kitchen but there was nothing there with Mary's phone number on it. Amongst the recipes clipped from magazines, the council tax bill, out of date vouchers and free samples of face cream were scraps of paper with phone numbers written on – the doctor, the dentist, the school, and Ramona's mobile phone, the one Tilly had bought her when she started secondary school. But there was no number for Mary. There were no numbers programmed into the landline phone; Tilly never bothered with that sort of thing. Mary's number would be in her grandmother's head, and that was enough, and she wouldn't need to have her best friend's address written down because she could find the house blindfolded.

Anyway, even if Ramona did have Mary's phone number, she couldn't phone her, could she? She'd imagined the conversation, how it might go if she'd got this all wrong. Mary might say Tilly wasn't at her house and she hadn't been expecting her today. And then she would want to know why Ramona was asking, and she wouldn't have an answer to that. Not the right answer, because there wouldn't have been one.

Too late, Ramona would have alerted somebody to the problem – not that it *was* a problem, more of a plain fact – that her grandmother was temporarily missing. Naturally, Mary would ask her to ring and let her know when Tilly turned up, and if by any chance she hadn't, Mary would take over. She'd come over to Number One The Pasture and before Ramona could draw breath, Mary would alert the police, all hell would break loose and the whole thing would run out of control.

If Tilly then turned up with some perfectly innocent explanation, or the police tracked her down, she'd be told off for leaving a twelve-year-old on her own for so long, and before Ramona knew which way was up, she'd be whisked away and stuck in a home with strangers.

Ramona's mind flew back to a conversation she'd had with Tilly; she didn't know how old she'd been at the time, but old enough to ask questions about her mother, and about how she came to be living with her grandparents. This was before her grandfather, Dennis, had fallen off his bike on the way to the allotment and died because he'd hit his head in the wrong place.

Tilly and Dennis had sat Ramona down and explained everything in a way that she'd understand. And she had understood, all of it. Especially the bit where her grandparents had nearly been stopped from taking Ramona after her mother had died, not long after giving birth to her. They'd had to face all sorts of questions, talk to loads of officials, and it had been touch and go at one point. Tilly and Dennis had put up quite a fight before they'd been allowed to take Ramona home and bring her up.

She was ever grateful to them, and lucky, too, she knew that. If things had all gone wrong at the start, she'd have been taken into what they called 'care' and her life would have turned out very differently.

Oh yes, Ramona knew how the system worked, and she was having no part of it. They might even come and take her away *before* Tilly came home. Think how upset she'd be to find Ramona gone and the police waiting to arrest her! She must carry on as usual and make the best she could of her new situation until Tilly came home and everything went back to normal. Her gran would expect no less of her.

With nobody to talk to, Ramona passed the evening by doing her maths homework, watching more telly, and reorganising her collection of animal bones.

Then she went to bed.

It gave Ramona a funny sensation in her stomach when she checked her grandmother's room first thing in the morning and found the bed empty. If this was Tilly giving Ramona her independence, she wasn't doing it by halves, was she?

The world around her seemed to have tilted slightly in the night; nothing felt quite as steady as it had been before.

Standing in Tilly's bedroom, she looked around at the familiar things: the pale green walls, framed pictures of the Swiss mountains, sheep in a field and a bright, modern painting of some sort of market, somewhere. She looked at the little china dishes on top of the chest which held odds and ends of jewellery, the photo of her grandfather on the bedside table, the black velvety slippers under a white-painted wooden chair, and Tilly's duvet cover, its pink flowers all smoothed out from when the bed was last made. At least nothing in here had changed. All Tilly's things were quietly waiting for her. Ramona opened the window a fraction to let the air in, then went downstairs.

She remembered Lilah was waiting for her to get in touch about going out this morning, and thumbed a quick text explaining that Tilly needed her at home and they'd talk later. Lilah's reply came back just as fast. *Ok no worries.* Then a row of emojis featuring, for some weird reason, dogs and a camel. Ramona didn't feel guilty; Lilah would line up Mila or one of their other friends to go out with. There'd be no shortage of takers for a Saturday morning trip to Lewes or Cliffhaven. Anything to relieve the boredom of sticking around at home.

Ramona felt only the tiniest flash of jealousy as she picked up the landline phone and dialled 1471. She might have missed a call while she'd been sleeping; it was possible. But the last call had been on Wednesday, from Ramona herself.

A short while later, showered and dressed, she sat in the kitchen and ate a bowl of cereal. It settled her stomach but used up all the milk. Tilly would be dying for a cup of tea when she got home. That would be the first thing she'd want, as well as toast and marmalade. There was no bread either. Ramona took a five-pound note and some coins from the housekeeping jar, locked up and set out for the village shop in the high street, remembering to leave a note for Tilly in case she returned in the meantime.

The village shop was laid out like a supermarket, only smaller. The rows between the shelves were so narrow you had to stand sideways to let other people pass. Tilly was always complaining about it. Ramona picked up a wire basket and collected the milk, bread and a box of her favourite cereal; she wasn't keen on the substitute one the online people had sent.

There were probably other supplies they needed – she'd not had a chance to take stock yet – but she couldn't think about that now. Adding a six-pack of Penguins and a bag of apples to the basket, she joined the queue at the till.

Nobody seemed to be in a hurry, which was just as well as the shop owner who was serving was taking an age. Ramona tapped her feet on the rubber mat and changed the basket from one hand to the other.

Other shoppers were chatting as they waited. 'Well, I do hope she's all right,' Ramona heard a woman say from the front of the queue. 'If I'd have thought, I could have gone in the ambulance with her, poor soul. She had nobody else by the looks of it.'

'You did right,' the man behind the counter said, his voice gruff. 'You could've been down that hospital all day, waiting about in A&E. You did your bit, ringing the ambulance. They'd have contacted somebody to be with Mrs Donnelly, sooner or later. It was only a fainting turn, most like. Dizzy spell or summat. They've probably sent her home by now. They don't bung up the beds with fainting old ladies. They haven't got the space.'

'No, they certainly haven't,' somebody else said. 'They've not got enough beds for those in real need, or the staff to look after them. It's shocking, it is.'

'Shocking,' someone else agreed. 'Time the government did something.'

Ramona's mind was focussed on the earlier part of the conversation. *Mrs Donnelly?* They were talking about Tilly, they must be. They couldn't mean another Mrs Donnelly; it was too much of a coincidence. Her neck prickled and her heartbeat picked up speed. She leaned round the queue for a better look at who was at the front. It was a tallish woman with shoulder length chestnut hair. She had a slim figure and a pretty face.

Ramona couldn't think who the woman reminded her of for a moment, and then it came to her. The woman looked exactly like the weather girl on tea-time telly. It wasn't her, of course – it couldn't be – but she was so much like her. Ramona's whole body lurched forwards of its own accord, almost cannoning into the man in front of her, and then it lurched back again as her brain sorted itself out and she remembered, just in time, that she must keep quiet and not let anyone know she was on her own at home.

'I'm expect you're right,' Weather Girl was saying, lifting her bag of shopping off the counter. 'It was probably the heat that got to her. It's been awfully oppressive lately.'

'Oh, it has,' somebody else said. 'Doesn't seem right to complain about summery weather when we get so little of it, but it makes me sluggish. And as for the nights, I hardly get a wink, it's so stuffy!'

There were murmurs of agreement as they went on talking about the weather. Ramona listened hard but nobody mentioned Tilly again. She thought about asking what it was they'd said about a lady being taken away in an ambulance, but she didn't know any of these people and it was best not to draw attention to herself.

She needed to be out of the shop and home, as fast as possible. The queue continued to move forward at a snail's pace and Ramona was fast running out of patience when finally she reached the counter. Her purchases stuffed into a carrier bag, she half-jogged, half speed-walked home, her forehead breaking out in a sweat. If Tilly arrived home by ambulance, she needed to be there to take care of her and make her tea and toast.

The ambulance didn't come, and neither did Tilly.

Ramona held out for an hour before she looked up the

number on her phone and rang Cliffhaven General. It was the nearest hospital; there wasn't another one. After an age, the ringing stopped and she thought she must have been cut off. And then, just as she was about to ring off and start again, a woman with a tired voice answered. Ramona apologised for disturbing her before she asked about Tilly.

'Hold on,' the woman said, and after more waiting, another female voice asked how she could help, and Ramona repeated her enquiry.

'Donnelly, you said?'

'Yes, Tilly Donnelly. Well, Matilda, really. Is this the right place to ask?'

'It is. She's with us. Mrs Donnelly is poorly but stable. We're keeping her under observation and she'll be undergoing tests. And you are?'

'Me? Oh, I'm not anybody. I was in the shop when she was taken ill. I got the ambulance to come. I just wanted to know how she was, that's all.'

'Oh, right.' The woman, who must be a nurse, Ramona thought, sounded disappointed. 'I hoped you might be a relative. Mrs Donnelly's not making much sense but she keeps asking for Caroline. You don't know who that is, I suppose?'

Ramona's heart banged like a gong. 'No, I don't,' she said, crossing her fingers behind back. 'I'm sorry.'

'We don't usually give out information on patients, only to close relatives. But if you've any idea who this Caroline is and where we can get in touch with her we'd be grateful to hear. Just give us a call back.'

The phone went dead.

Caroline. Ramona's mother. She had no memories of her but the link was there, all the same. A deep, almost tangible connection. Unbreakable. A part of her, forever.

Ramona swallowed away the lump that had risen in her

throat. Why would Tilly be asking for her daughter when she'd died over twelve years ago? Tilly knew that, of course she did. She couldn't have forgotten something so vital, however ill she was. Perhaps they hadn't heard her properly at the hospital, and she hadn't said 'Caroline' at all. It wasn't an easy name to mistake, though, was it?

For the first time since Tilly went missing, Ramona's lip trembled, and she felt the sting of tears. She wouldn't let them fall. She had to stay strong for Tilly, and believe she'd get better quickly. She reminded herself what the people in the shop had said, that she'd fainted because of the heat. In that case, she'd be home soon. And – Ramona drew on her store of logic – if she wasn't, they had phones in the hospital, didn't they? Tilly would ring and let her know when she would be home, or if she couldn't ring herself, she would ask that nurse to do it for her. And Ramona would be here and have everything ready for when Tilly *did* come home.

CHAPTER 4

'What time are we eating tonight?' Emily leaned in to kiss Ethan but found only air as he sidestepped her and opened the back door, ready to leave.

'Tonight?' He looked nonplussed for a split second before the expression vanished, causing Emily wonder if she'd imagined it. 'Ah, yes. Dinner at The Walnut Tree. Looking forward to it.' He smiled, a little distractedly.

'D'you still want to go out tonight? Only, it's fine if you don't.' Ethan didn't seem too sure. She wasn't going to press him into a date if he wasn't up for it.

'Of course.' He looked almost affronted that she'd asked. 'I've booked a table for eight o'clock. I told you, didn't I?'

Well, no, he hadn't. She'd have remembered. That was why she was asking. A weirdly formal vibe had somehow crept into the conversation, as if it was taking place between two other people, people who didn't know each other very well.

She rallied, cursing her overly analytical mind that served her well in her job as a newspaper reporter and journalist but could foist unnecessary complications on her personal relationships.

She and Ethan had just spent a wonderful night together, and tonight he was taking her out to dinner. What more could she want?

She smiled, stepping forward and placing her hand lightly on his chest, just below his shirt collar. 'Great. Will you come here first, or shall I meet you at the restaurant?'

'No, I'll pick you up. Quarter to eight, or thereabouts.'

'Okay.'

'See you later. Have a good day.' She tried to sound light and casual. It took more effort than it should have.

'You too.' Ethan brushed her mouth with his, then he was gone.

She closed the back door of Cloud Cottage and leaned against it for a moment, feeling a vague sense of disappointment. She had hoped they'd spend the rest of the day together as it was Sunday. Perhaps she should have expressed that hope last night instead of leaving it to chance. But then she'd have sounded needy, a quality she deplored in other women and not something she was about to start now.

Peeling away from the door, she picked up a leftover triangle of cold toast from the plate and bit into it, her thoughts turning to Ethan's day. Sunday or not, he'd obviously planned to work, at least for part of it, although he hadn't said so specifically, and she hadn't asked. She'd woken early to the sound of the shower, then watched him dress rapidly, as if he couldn't wait to be away. So, yes, he clearly had work to do, work he enjoyed, and she was glad about that.

Ethan worked long, irregular hours as a graphic designer. It was his own business, started up partly with an inheritance from an uncle. In Emily's opinion, gleaned from the relatively little information he'd given her, he'd taken on too many contracts. He couldn't afford to turn them down, he said, while he was still establishing himself, having worked in London for a large design company until he branched out on his own. He wasn't entirely on his own – he had a small team of freelancers he could call on. But still, Emily understood the pressures.

Ethan lived and worked in the same place, an airy apartment overlooking Brighton Marina, chosen for its location – he liked to look at the sea – and the light that poured in through the picture windows. Living 'over the shop', as he called it, meant that the lines between his work and home life weren't clearly defined.

Emily sometimes worked at the weekend, too, if there was an event she needed to attend or a story that couldn't wait. Unsocial hours went with the territory and she was used to it, as Ethan obviously was. Even so, somehow she found it difficult to imagine him spending his Sunday slaving over a hot drawing board. The distractions of the marina on a beautiful day like this must be hard to resist.

Which Emily, apparently, wasn't.

She opened the back door and went outside before the unwelcome thought took hold and ran away with itself.

They'd had an enjoyable dinner out here on the patio last night – salmon, salad and new potatoes, followed by strawberry tarts from the bakery, an easy meal they'd prepared together, working companionably side by side in the cottage's tiny kitchen. Later, when the stars pierced the clear sky above the deep purple shadows of the South Downs and the night air brushed, cashmere-soft, against her bare shoulders, Ethan had cajoled her, in that gentle, funny way of his, into taking the remains of the bottle of wine up to bed. She hadn't needed much cajoling. She hadn't even faked resistance. She was too old to play games.

It was still ridiculously early. The leaves held fat drops of dew, and the grass beneath her bare feet felt cool and moist. Emily picked a perfect pink rose and held it to her face, breathing in the sweetness from the damp petals. Back in the kitchen, she ran water into a slender glass vase, dropped the flower in, and stood it on the windowsill. Ethan's watch was there, where he'd left it last night while he'd rinsed the wine glasses in the sink. She picked it up and gazed into its expensive, subtly shimmering face. The watch had been a present from his father for his fortieth birthday, he'd told her.

That was seven years back. She hadn't known him then, of course. He'd walked into her life, and her heart, five months ago, in the car park of the Cliffhaven News. He'd been heading into the office for a meeting about advertising space, she'd been on her way out to a routine reporting assignment. Having set eyes on each other, neither had been in a hurry to go anywhere.

Five months. Okay, it wasn't long in the great scheme of things, but at times their relationship had a kind of static feel about it. Taking things slowly was probably for the best, though, considering her love life so far was peppered with unwise choices.

That wasn't strictly fair; she had to take some of the blame, if not all it, when it came to failed relationships, some of which had never got off the starting blocks before it was obvious she'd got it wrong, again.

Her twelve year marriage to Mitch wasn't a mistake – she could never think of it that way. They'd fallen in love with incredible speed and married within months of meeting, a textbook whirlwind romance. She had loved him, truly, and he her. They'd been happy, delighting in one another more as time went on. But they'd fallen apart almost as fast as they'd got together, which had come as a surprise to them both before they were forced to accept that the emotional gap between them was so wide that it was obvious there was no way back. By then, Mitch had met somebody else. Despite their differences, Emily should by rights have been heartbroken but she wasn't, which was when the writing went up on the wall, in foot high neon letters.

She'd wished Mitch well, still did, wherever he was. He was a lovely man – mostly. Just not *her* lovely man, in the end.

In her darkest moments – who didn't experience those, from time to time? – she wondered if she was lacking in some vital way that made her difficult to love. Impossible, even. Deep down, though, she knew it wasn't true. She valued herself more highly than that.

So where were these feelings about Ethan coming from? On the face of it, he'd done nothing wrong, nothing to hurt her. He had told her he loved her, and she had said it back. Wasn't that all there was, all there needed to be, for now? It was just that occasionally, like this morning, she sensed a distance, as if there was a part of him, a secret side, she had no access to.

She was probably expecting too much. She was overthinking it; that was usually her problem.

Walking through to the sitting room, she took her laptop to the sofa and opened her work emails. But it was still the weekend; she didn't need to be doing this today. She wasn't in the mood, and a first look told her there was nothing that couldn't wait until tomorrow, when she'd be back in the office. Closing the laptop and setting it aside, her mind drifted back to the events of Friday and that unfortunate incident in the village shop.

CHAPTER 5

The scene around the woman who'd collapsed had threatened to descend into chaos as people gathered around, anxious to help or at least give an opinion. But nobody, it seemed, had actually sent for help, and Emily had taken charge and rung for an ambulance. Well, somebody had to. The general consensus was that she'd simply fainted from the heat, which may have been the case, but you couldn't take chances in a situation like that, especially with an older person.

The woman's name was Matilda Donnelly, according to Don, the shop owner, and nobody had cause to doubt it, since practically the whole village had crossed his threshold constantly, over the years. Other customers had chipped in with snippets of information, all of which seemed random and plucked out of thin air, if Emily was any judge.

Matilda Donnelly lived alone, apparently. That much everyone agreed on, although nobody seemed to know whereabouts. Her smooth complexion and the classic, short-layered cut of her silvery hair had made it difficult to estimate her age, but Emily guessed at late seventies or a well-preserved eighty. The woman's blue eyes as she'd focussed on Emily while she stooped beside her had an intensity about them, as if she was trying to convey a message but couldn't find the words.

With everything that had gone on, Emily had left the shop on Friday with only half the items she'd needed and she'd returned yesterday morning. Don had served her again, and while the queue built up, the chat had turned briefly to Mrs Donnelly and her collapse, or faint, whatever it had been, but nobody had any news.

Matilda Donnelly had returned to Emily's mind this morning as she'd watched Ethan eating toast standing up, his mug of tea in the other hand.

'Why are you worrying about some old dear who collapsed in the shop?' he'd asked, plainly puzzled by her concern. 'You don't know her, do you?'

'No, but isn't that how it starts, loneliness? People finding themselves completely cut off because everybody said the same, "Nothing to do with me." That's so sad.'

Ethan had laughed, but kindly. 'You're too soft for your own good, Em. Quit with the worrying and let somebody else do it.'

As long as there *was* somebody else.

Ethan was right, though. She didn't know Matilda Donnelly. All the same, that searching, almost urgent, look she'd seen in the woman's eyes as she lay helpless on the shop floor had triggered something deeper than plain curiosity. She'd been tempted to go with Matilda in the ambulance but again Ethan was right; she was nothing to do with her, and the woman might not have appreciated having a stranger by her side.

Even so, she would like to know how the patient was, and whether she'd already made it home safely to Charnley Acre. There was only one way to find out. She went to the kitchen, made a mug of coffee and rang Cliffhaven General on her mobile. It took a while for anyone to answer, and then it was another age before she was put through to the right ward.

Emily sipped her coffee while she waited.

Understandably, the nurse, or whoever eventually answered, wanted to know who she was. Emily explained her tenuous connection to Matilda Donnelly, and fully expected to be sent away empty-handed. But no.

'Ah, you're the person who rang yesterday,' a bright voice said. 'I'm the ward sister. You spoke to me.'

Wrongfooted, Emily was silent for a moment before admitting she hadn't rung before. Lying wouldn't serve any useful purpose. She just wanted to know if Mrs Donnelly was still on the ward, she explained, and if so, how she was. If that's possible, she added apologetically.

'Oh, sorry, my mistake. I thought you must be the same person I spoke to, although now I think about it, she sounded a bit younger... Anyway, while you're on, I don't suppose you know of anyone called Caroline, do you? She could be a relative. Mrs Donnelly keeps insisting that there's somebody called Caroline who's coming to fetch her. Actually, that was yesterday. She's not had a lucid moment so far this morning.'

'No, I'm sorry, I don't know anything about her relatives,' Emily said. 'I wish I could help but I'm just a concerned neighbour. Is her condition serious? You might not be allowed to tell me, I realise that, but I really would like to know how she is.'

'A collapse is always potentially serious with a lady of her age. We don't have a full diagnosis, she's still undergoing tests, or she will be, tomorrow. We're keeping her here for the time being. That's as much as I can tell you, I'm afraid. Actually, we don't know much more ourselves yet.'

'That's fine,' Emily said. 'Well, obviously it's not fine that she's poorly, but she's in the right place, and I promise if I find out anything I'll let you know.'

The call ended, Emily tipped the cold dregs of her coffee into the sink. At least Mrs Donnelly was in safe hands; she'd found out that much. But who had rung the hospital yesterday with the same query? She couldn't think it was anyone who'd been in the shop at the time. People had been concerned, of course, but only in a detached sort of way. The ward sister might have made a mistake and confused the two enquiries. They were so busy, she wouldn't be surprised.

A little later, Emily clicked shut the front gate of Cloud Cottage and set off along Hammerpot Lane for a roundabout walk to the village. She was in no hurry. Ethan wasn't due till tonight. Until then, the day was hers.

Skirting the common, then the woods and fields where grazing cows lazily lifted their heads to gaze at her as she passed, she emerged from the twitten that brought her into the high street. The village shop opened for a couple of hours on Sunday mornings as it sold newspapers. Picking up a paper from the rack outside, Emily went in to pay. There was no sign of Don but his wife, Pauline, was behind the counter. Emily relayed her conversation with the ward sister at Cliffhaven General, including the part about somebody called Caroline who, it seemed, could be a relative or close friend of their new patient.

Pauline gave a regretful shake of her head. 'At one time, the whole village knew everything about everybody, including their shoe size, but not now. Anyway, those who did know the poor old soul have most likely passed on already.'

Pauline delivered this gloomy prediction with a cheery, lightness of tone that made Emily laugh.

'You make her sound about a hundred. I didn't think she looked that ancient, even in that state.'

'I didn't see her myself, did I? I was having my roots done at the salon, missed all the excitement. It was Don told me she'd taken a tumble, right by the cereals. Shame for her.'

Emily hid a smile. 'Nobody seemed to know exactly where Mrs Donnelly lives, only that she's definitely from Charnley Acre. I don't suppose you know, do you?'

Emily had no idea what she was going to do with the information if it was forthcoming, only that she thought it might come in useful at some point.

'Don asked me that. I've got it in the back of my mind she's not from right here in the village. Maybe up top, near the farm, somewhere like that?' Pauline waved a plump, freckled arm in a vague northerly direction. 'I could be making it up. I usually do,' she added, as Emily turned to leave. 'See you, love.'

'Yes, see you.'

Emily left the shop and continued her walk along the high street. Her thoughts about Matilda Donnelly dissolved completely as she came to a shop called We'll Meet Again, which sold good quality pre-owned clothes. The shop occupied a prime position, with the bakery on one side and the craft and gift shop on the other, also open today in the hope of catching visitors' attention. We'll Meet Again was a favourite with Emily and her best friend, Laura Engleby. The two of them, sometimes with Laura's daughter, Holly, often spent a happy Saturday morning browsing the rails.

Emily peered in the window to check out what was new, cupping her hands to the glass to see beyond the reflection. She sensed movement behind the display and, a moment later, the shop door opened and Nikki, the owner, gave a welcoming smile.

'Emily! Coming in?'

'Oh, I didn't realise you were open,' Emily said, stepping towards her.

'I don't often open on a Sunday but it's such a lovely day and there'll be visitors about. I'd hate to disappoint them.' She gathered her long blonde hair into a ponytail and fixed it with a band from her wrist. 'Mind you, I've been dead quiet so far. Coffee's on.' She raised her eyebrows pointedly at Emily.

'Well, we can't have it going to waste,' Emily said, laughing as she followed Nikki into the shop.

The aroma of freshly-made coffee greeted her, mixed enticingly with the scent of a small vase of freesias that sat on the counter. Nikki treated her customers well, and anyone showing the slightest interest in the clothes was offered a free coffee. It meant, of course, that those who'd only come in to browse, or so they'd thought, might spot something they really had to try on while they lingered over their coffee. Nikki was a great salesperson; Emily had always admired her for it.

Nikki poured them both coffees from the jug. Emily sat down on a pink velvet stool in front of the curtained changing room while Nikki leaned against the counter.

'That's called no-obligation coffee, by the way.' She nodded towards Emily's paper cup.

Emily laughed. 'Funny way to shift stock if you ask me.'

'You're one of my best customers. I'll let you off as it's Sunday. Just out for a stroll, are you?'

'Yep, and to grab a paper.' Emily indicated the folded Telegraph sticking out of her bag.

And to probe the mystery of Matilda Donnelly a little further, Emily thought, recalling her conversation with Pauline. But she'd done with that for now. There was nothing more she could do to help, that was obvious.

'Actually, I love that dress in the window. I couldn't see it properly from outside but from here it's gorgeous. Can I have a look?'

'Sure.' Nikki soon had the dress out of the display and was holding it up for Emily to see. 'It's your size, too. Want to try it on?'

The dress was a simple linen shift, sleeveless, with a notched neckline, in the same beautiful blue-green as the far-out sea when the light was on it. Moments later, Emily was behind the velvet curtain in the fitting room, stepping into the dress.

'The colour goes wonderfully with your chestnut hair,' Nikki said, standing behind Emily as she admired her reflection. 'That's the truth, by the way, not sales talk.'

They both laughed.

Nikki was right, though; the dress flattered her colouring and her figure. She could wear it tonight when they went to The Walnut Tree. Linen would be cool and comfortable on a warm evening.

Declining another coffee, Emily chatted with Nikki while the sale was completed. She carried her purchase home to Cloud Cottage, a lightness in her step as she looked forward to her date with Ethan.

CHAPTER 6

Ramona spent Sunday morning cleaning and tidying the house. She made a special effort with Tilly's bedroom, even remembering to flick the feather duster along the skirting boards and around the picture frames. The room hadn't been dirty to begin with but Tilly would need to rest. She'd hate her to come home to a dusty bedroom, and it wasn't worth taking any chances.

There was none of the stuff left that Tilly used to clean the bath and basin, at least, none that she could find, but a swish round with the sponge dipped in washing-up liquid seemed to do the trick. She didn't bother brushing or hoovering the stairs. They were so awkward, with the narrowness and the twisty bit near the top. But overall, she was satisfied with the way things looked, once, she'd finished.

The next question was what to have for dinner. Tilly usually did a roast on Sunday. Ramona felt hunger pangs just thinking about it. But that kind of cooking was beyond her, even if she'd had the ingredients, and would take too long anyway. She inspected the contents of the fridge and freezer. The online supermarket delivery might have failed on the cereal front, and there was only a scraping of butter left as that hadn't been sent either, but there were chicken fillets, fresh in a packet, in the fridge, a lump of pinkish meat that was labelled 'pork shoulder' and two big packs of mince. Tilly made lots of tasty dinners with mince, but Ramona had no idea how to go about cooking it, so she moved the mince from the fridge to the freezer, as well as the pork and chicken, so none of it would go off before Tilly got home.

There were vegetables in the wire rack, but other than microwaving a potato, she wasn't sure what to do with those, so she pushed the rack back in and hoped nothing would go mouldy too quickly.

But all was not lost; there were eggs in the fridge, and bacon. She'd fried things before, under Tilly's close instruction. How hard could it be? Ramona got the frying pan out and tipped in a little oil, remembering Tilly's warning not to use too much or it would spatter.

In the end, it was quite a nice Sunday dinner, not what she was used to but she'd managed not to set fire to the kitchen. A good result, Ramona thought, as she ate, even though she'd had to open the window to let out the fug from the frying, which let in a draught.

Her dinner things cleared away and washed up, Ramona began to worry again about Tilly, how she was feeling, and whether she'd been given a good Sunday dinner. Meals in hospitals weren't always up to scratch, Ramona had heard. And then, once she'd started worrying, a black hole opened up in her mind, threatening to suck her in and not let go for the rest of the day. She couldn't let that happen. Tilly was in a safe place, being cared for; that was all she needed to remember.

Diversion was the thing; something to take her mind off the situation was obviously what she needed. She fetched her English Lit set book from upstairs and settled down in the living room to read. She'd got a bit behind with the book, which wasn't surprising considering everything else she'd had to think about. Plus, *Northanger Abbey* wasn't exactly a page-turner, Jane Austen or not. But she ploughed on through fifteen deadly pages, then smiled with relief when a text came through on her phone from Lilah.

The messages pinged back and forth about a million times, *Northanger Abbey* lying forgotten on the floor. As she thumbed in her replies to Lilah's texts, which were mostly to do with Jamie Tate in their year, and didn't Ramona agree he looked exactly like some film actor or other? As Ramona had never heard of the actor, she could only agree. If Lilah had developed a crush on Jamie – and it certainly seemed that way – it could get awfully boring. But Lilah was her bestie, and it was her job to listen and respond in the right way.

By the time the messages stopped, Ramona began to feel more cheerful. Lilah's last text before she announced she had to go was a string of daft emojis. Ramona responded similarly, then got up from the chair and wondered what to do with herself for the rest of the day.

Tucked away in a corner of a field, the cottage was quiet – always, not just because it was Sunday. She'd never minded before. But now... She looked at Tilly's empty chair, the silence heavy around her. Perhaps she should go for a walk. But the sun had gone in ages ago, and she wasn't in the mood. Anyway, she really ought to stay at home in case Tilly or the hospital phoned, or the ambulance came with Tilly in it. Ramona put the TV on, found a film she'd seen before and settled down to wait.

Nobody phoned. The ambulance didn't come.

Ramona wasn't really surprised. There might not be many nurses on duty at the weekend, and Tilly might not have been able to ask to use the phone. The doctors may not have done their usual rounds, either, which meant it was unlikely they'd let Tilly out today.

In her heart, Ramona knew she was inventing reasons for her grandmother's continued absence. There again, there had to *be* a reason; it was just that she had no way of knowing what it was. She thought about phoning the hospital again but decided against it in case she was asked any awkward questions.

She'd just have to be patient – they both would. Tilly must be as anxious to be sent home as Ramona was to receive her.

Sunday had been the longest day *ever* in the whole of her life, Ramona decided. The usual Monday morning scurry of washing and dressing, having breakfast, gathering her stuff together and rushing to the bus stop was a relief. By the time the bus arrived and Ramona hopped on, joining the little group from the village who went to her school, it felt almost as if this was an ordinary day.

At first break, she rang home from her mobile, then tried again during the dinner break. There was no answer either time. Number One The Pasture was still clearly unoccupied.

It didn't matter, Ramona told herself, as she joined the throng in the corridor on the way to the lab for double science, Lilah nattering away in her ear about nothing in particular. Tilly was fine, wasn't she? She was having tests, she remembered the nurse saying that now. They'd have to wait for the results before they decided she was well enough to be discharged, making sure, being cautious. That was surely a good thing, and would definitely take time. Meanwhile, all Ramona had to do was sit tight and keep everything ticking away, as normal.

Tilly liked normal. She didn't like change or surprises. It didn't mean she was stuck in her ways, or really old-fashioned or anything. It was just how she was, as Ramona had sussed out years ago. Thinking about this side of her gran's character, she began to worry again, just a bit. Hospital was change – mega change – and the way Tilly had ended up there when she'd only popped out to do some shopping must have come as a big surprise. But Tilly was also strong and sensible. She would understand that whatever tests and treatment she was having was for the best, so that was all right.

At the end of school, as Ramona was walking to the bus stop with a group of friends, three boys from her class pushed past, dead close to them, which was *so* annoying. The boys were yelling and laughing, and making stupid remarks. As they jostled Ramona's group on purpose, she found herself being knocked sideways, into Lilah. The girls laughed, Ramona among them, although she didn't much feel like laughing. Ramona noticed Lilah was blushing a bit, presumably because one of the boys was Jamie Tate. She definitely had a big crush on him. Ramona pretended she hadn't noticed the blush. If it was she who liked somebody, she wouldn't want to be teased about it, although whoever fancied any of that lot needed their bumps tested.

At the bus-stop, Lilah suddenly turned to Ramona.

'Hey, don't get your bus. Come back to tea at ours. Your gran won't mind, will she?'

Ramona hesitated as the possible complications crossed her mind. 'I should get home, really.'

'Oh no, go on!' Lilah was practically dancing on the pavement as she grabbed Ramona's arm. 'I didn't see you on Saturday. Ring your gran now and ask her.'

It would be a relief not to have to get her own meal tonight, and it would be all right because Tilly wasn't likely to be sent home this late in the day – well, she *could* be, but it was a chance worth taking, Ramona decided.

'Okay.' Taking her phone out of her bag, she stepped away

from Lilah and turned her back on her. When she glanced round, Lilah was chatting to somebody else, but Ramona acted as if the call was genuine, just in case. 'Yes... okay.... Mm, will do. Bye Tilly.'

She returned to Lilah, her fingers crossed by her side. She hated lying, but needs must. 'She said it's fine as long as I get the seven o'clock bus home at the latest.' *Exactly what Tilly would have said*. Ramona was getting good at this.

'Great. Come on, then.' Lilah linked her arm with Ramona's and they set off.

There were three bikes, two footballs, and a bent hula-hoop abandoned on the scrubby grass in Lilah's front garden, as well as a trowel stuck in the soil and a battered cardboard box with weeds in where someone had had a go at the borders. Ramona loved coming here. Lilah had four brothers and a sister, and the house was always full of noise and chaos. It made a change from the quiet of home, and Lilah's mum didn't mind who turned up for meals because she always cooked loads.

Tonight, it was sausages, mash, cabbage and tinned sweetcorn. Ramona squeezed onto a stool at the table between Lilah and one of her older brothers.

As Lilah's mum put her heaped plate in front of her, she gave her a wide, warm smile. 'Nice to see you, darlin'. Tuck in, don't wait or it'll get cold.'

By the time the apple crumble and custard was served and everyone had finished, there was only half an hour left for Ramona and Lilah to spend together because of the fake bus curfew. They'd been together all day, of course, but they were in different sets for some subjects, and Ramona had disappeared for a while at lunchtime while she phoned home.

Upstairs, Lilah gave her sister, Sophie, a mini-sized bag of

Maltesers and ordered her out of the bedroom they shared. The little girl flounced off with a dramatic eye roll.

'So, look, if Jamie asks me out and I say yes, can I say I'm at your house?' Lilah unhooked her school skirt, letting it fall to the floor.

'Is that the only reason you invited me, so you could persuade me to be your alibi?' Ramona crossed her arms, pretending to be annoyed.

Lilah laughed. 'Yeah, what else?' She nodded towards the door. 'Keep your voice down, will you?'

'Seriously, though,' Ramona began, wriggling herself onto the windowsill between the piles of jigsaw puzzles, books and soft toys. 'We're only twelve. That's too young to go out with boys.'

Lilah tugged her school shirt over her head without undoing the buttons and dropped it on the floor. The rest of her uniform followed. 'We're not that far off thirteen. We'll be teenagers soon. Anyway, Simone in our class has got a boyfriend.'

'Simone is Simone.'

'What's that supposed to mean?' Lilah wriggled into a black T-shirt dress that ended halfway down her thighs.

Ramona wouldn't wear something like that – not that Tilly would let her – but somehow it looked good on Lilah, with her long blonde hair and slim figure that was clearly maturing at a faster rate than Ramona's.

'It *means* everyone is different, and what is right for one person isn't necessarily right for somebody else.'

'Trust you to add another complication.' Lilah rolled her eyes. 'So, can I say I'm at yours or not?'

'*If* Jamie asks you out. You don't know he's going to.'

'One likes to be prepared, you know?' Lilah struck a comical model pose, one hand behind her head. They both giggled.

Ramona thought for a moment. 'Your mum doesn't know Tilly, so I guess it would work.'

'Ta. I knew you'd see sense.'

'I never *actually* said I'd do it....'

'You will, though.' Lilah smiled.

'I will. Most probably,' Ramona said.

'*Most probably*. You're funny. Anway, why do you call her Tilly, not Gran or Nan, like other people do?'

Ramona shrugged. 'I don't know. I just do. You don't have to look for reasons in everything.'

'*I do*.' Lilah flopped down on her bed. The dress rode up another couple of inches, nearly as far as her knickers. Ramona wore short skirts – everyone did – but she couldn't imagine getting away with one that short. Tilly would have a blue fit.

They chatted a bit more, thankfully not about Jamie Tate, which could get seriously boring, until Lilah's mum yelled up the stairs that it was ten to seven. Ramona slid off the windowsill and almost fell over one of Lilah's brothers as she hurtled down the stairs and out of the front door.

It was only when she reached the bus stop and stuck her arm out as the bus approached that she remembered she'd made up the thing about having to catch the seven o'clock bus and it wouldn't have mattered if she'd taken her time and got the next one.

Funny, wasn't it, how you could invent a story and end up believing it yourself?

After Lilah's house the cottage seemed extra quiet and the field it stood in suddenly seemed like the loneliest place in the world, as if nobody ever set foot in it, which they didn't much, apart from the man from the farm who drove the mower around it occasionally.

Ramona thought about how much she missed Tilly, and how horrible it must be for her being stuck in the hospital, waiting for the doctors to let her come home. She began to feel as if she might have a little cry. But what good would that do either of them?

Another thought arrived in her head before she could stop it. Had she made a mistake, not telling anyone she'd been left alone? Had she got this all wrong? And then she reminded herself why she was doing this, and how horrible it would be if the social people wouldn't let Tilly look after her any more. It would break Tilly's heart, as well as Ramona's, and she wouldn't let that happen.

No, she just had to carry on until things worked themselves out, which they would, very soon. As Lilah had reminded her, she was very nearly a teenager. She wasn't stupid; she could look after herself.

She did her history homework without putting the TV on, even though Tilly wasn't there to see. Then she started up the laptop Tilly had bought for them to share, and logged on to the bank account.

Tilly had got to grips with using a computer really quickly, once they'd acquired one, and Ramona used one at school, of course. The two of them had sat down and worked out together how to run the bank account, and the rest of the household admin, as Tilly called it. But for quite a while now, Ramona had been the one to do what was needed, including the online supermarket shop from Tilly's handwritten list. Tilly had talked about it being a good life experience for Ramona to take on these things, which she supposed it was, and if it helped her grandmother, Ramona had no problem with it. Except that Tilly seemed to have lost some of her confidence in carrying out tasks that she'd taken in her stride before. Ramona had noticed that, and wondered what it meant.

As she'd expected, the account seemed to be in order. The boring bills had been paid out of her grandmother's two pensions and other bits of money that arrived in the account – Ramona wasn't sure where from, probably because she had not paid attention at that point, not because Tilly hid anything from her. She told Ramona everything, always had. Which, in the situation Ramona found herself in now, was just as well.

Next, she looked in the housekeeping jar in the kitchen. There was enough cash to be going on with, but it wouldn't last forever. Luckily, Tilly's bank card lived in the same jar, and the PIN was pencilled on the back of a painting of a windmill in the hall, in case either of them forgot it. She could draw out more cash if she needed any before Tilly came home. There was never much money to spare, and by the time school stuff and clothes and bus fares had been paid for, the figure on the account had usually dwindled to almost nothing by the end of each month. But Tilly said they were ticking along nicely, and Ramona took her at her word.

One day at a time. Another of her grandmother's sayings. Well, that's what Ramona would do, take each day as it came.

But there was one thing she needed to find out which wouldn't wait. Not that there was anything to worry about yet, Tilly only having been gone three days and a bit, but it was best to keep on top of things, just in case.

Back at the laptop, she read lots of different articles about children with nobody at home to look after them and who the people were who had the biggest say in what happened to them. She had to use Google to find out what a 'minor' was, just to check that she was one, but other than that, there was nothing she didn't understand. In fact, she understood it all too well, and it firmed up her decision to keep quiet and tell nobody, not a living soul, that she was temporarily alone at Number One The Pasture.

There was no point inviting trouble.

Waking up alone in the morning had begun to feel almost normal. That was something else she'd learned; how quickly things became normal after quite a big change. Even so, Ramona switched the radio on to the local station, Cuckmere Sounds, while she got herself ready for school. She wasn't exactly listening, but it was better than silence.

During her tidying and cleaning session she'd collected up Tilly's four library books and left them in a neat pile on Tilly's chair. Seeing them again this morning, Ramona felt a twinge in her stomach, a sharp reminder of her gran's absence, as if she needed one. She'd definitely seen Tilly reading at least two of the books. The best thing she could do – the most helpful thing for Tilly – was to return them to the library. It would be one less thing for her gran to worry about when she got home.

Ramona ran her finger over the shiny plastic cover of the top book while she tried to remember whether the library opened on a Tuesday. She checked on her phone – it did, and didn't shut until five. As long as she didn't hang around after school she should make it.

The day seemed to go on forever – probably because she wasn't giving the lessons her full attention. She hadn't been able to concentrate, not even in biology and history, her favourite subjects. Tilly was always there, taking up a corner of her mind, which was only to be expected. But eventually, the final bell sounded and she dashed for the bus without waiting for Lilah, who could seriously hold you up if you weren't careful.

Back home, she changed her school uniform for jeans and a checked shirt, ran a brush through her hair and set off for the village with the books in a bag. The library was quiet, only one other person, an oldish man, roaming the shelves. Ramona's footsteps sounded loud as she walked up to the counter. There was one other person already there, and Ramona stepped aside and stood patiently, waiting for her turn. The woman at the counter was in deep conversation with the librarian, the short, square woman with pepper-and-salt curly hair whom Ramona had seen on previous visits. The woman she was talking to didn't seem to have any books with her, and Ramona hoped they weren't going to be much longer.

It suddenly came to her that there was something familiar about the woman; the way she tilted her head, her lovely chestnut hair. And then, as she turned a little, revealing more of her face, Ramona realised who it was – the woman who looked exactly like the weather girl on telly. She'd been in the village shop on Saturday, and she'd been talking about Tilly! That was how Ramona had found out about Tilly being taken to hospital.

Ramona blinked, and looked more closely. Yes, it was definitely her. Ramona's heart gave a little leap while her mind scrabbled through the options. It seemed as if was meant to be, this small, fragile connection with her grandmother appearing just when she needed one. She hadn't even realised she needed that, until now. Somehow, it made everything feel better.

The woman turned fully, spotted Ramona and smiled. 'Sorry, I'm holding you up, aren't I?' Then, turning back to the librarian: 'Let her duck in. I don't want to keep her waiting.'

Ramona smiled back. 'It's fine, honestly. I don't mind.'

But the librarian already had her hand out for the books and Ramona stepped up to the counter.

'Returning?'

'What? Oh, yes. Yes, please.'

The librarian checked her computer screen and peered at Ramona over the top of her glasses. 'There's one pound ninety to pay, I'm afraid. They're a touch overdue.'

It wasn't like Tilly to let her books go overdue. At least, it never used to be. She'd only brought the books back to be useful.

'Are you completely sure?' she asked, drawing herself up to her full height, which put her at least two inches above the librarian.

Weather girl seemed to be fighting off a smile. Well, she might take these things at face value, but Ramona didn't. The librarian looked amused, too. They could whistle, the both of them.

'Completely sure. These are adult books. They're not yours, are they? Weren't you sent with any money?'

Sent? Did she look like a five year old? Ramona drew in a sharp breath and moved closer to the counter, her knees pressing against the wood. 'First of all, I wasn't sent, I just came. And second, I forgot my purse. So, what shall I do? Take the books away and come back another day with the money?'

'No, no, for goodness sake, no.' The librarian's curls bobbed. 'They'll be even more overdue then. I'll write it down and you can see me next time.'

'If it helps,' Weather girl said, stepping in, 'I'll pay the fine. I'd be happy to, really.'

Ramona gave her a small, tight smile. She wasn't sure how she felt about the offer. It made her feel a bit stupid, as if she was a little kid. It was kind of her, though, wasn't it? But quite unnecessary. The matter of the fine was no longer uppermost in her mind; she was thinking about Tilly, and how this woman had almost gone in the ambulance with her.

The thread of connection grew a little bit stronger.

'I don't like being in debt,' Ramona said, holding her head up high. 'But if I have to, I'd rather be in debt to you than the library, because they need the money to buy more books with.'

Both women looked at one another. Their eyebrows had gone up a bit.

'In that case,' Weather Girl said, 'I'd be pleased to pay the fine, but I don't need you to pay me back, and then you, or whoever's books these are, wouldn't be in debt at all.'

Ramona's brain whirred. This was meant to be, wasn't it; an opportunity not to be wasted.

'Oh no, I must pay you back. Tell me where you live, and I'll drop the money in tomorrow. After school.'

'Will that be okay with your mum?'

'My...? Oh, yes. She'll be cross with herself letting the books go overdue. She'll want me to pay you back the money as soon as possible.'

Ramona didn't know why Weather-Girl and the librarian seemed to find everything she said funny. They tried to hide it, but she could tell. It was quite off-putting, really. But she'd achieved her aim and was being handed a library leaflet with the address scribbled on: Cloud Cottage, Hammerpot Lane. She knew exactly where it was; it was right by the common, just about the cutest cottage in Charnley Acre. It had a thatched roof and the prettiest garden, like a picture in a book.

'I'm Emily,' the woman said, smiling. She was doing a lot of that.

'I'm Ramona. I'm very pleased to meet you. I'll see you tomorrow, then. About half past four, if that's suitable.'

'Perfect,' Emily said.

CHAPTER 7

$\mathcal{I}$t was Tuesday evening and Emily was at Spindlewood, her friend Laura's wonderful old house with its quirky turret and extensive garden, situated half way up Charnley Hill. She spent almost as much time at Spindlewood as she did at Cloud Cottage.

'Come and keep me company,' Laura had said when she'd phoned. 'I'll feed you if you don't mind last night's lasagne reheated. I made double but Clayton's eating down at the Goose and Feather tonight with a mate of his.'

'Love to,' Emily had said. 'Reheated always tastes better.'

After they'd eaten, they'd taken the remains of a bottle of Malbec through to the sitting room, which was bathed in the soft golden light of a lowering sun.

'I can't believe he let you down again,' Laura said, topping up their glasses.

Emily had told Laura how Ethan had called off their dinner date on Sunday night. He'd sent a brief text – no phone call – two hours before he'd been due to pick her up, with a one-line apology but no real reason, just that 'something had come up' and he'd make it up to her. She'd waited half an hour before she'd texted back: 'OK. See you soon.' No kiss.

She hadn't told Laura she'd bought a new dress to wear to the Walnut Tree. She didn't know why, except she needed to keep intact the pride she had left where Ethan was concerned.

She flapped a hand, a throwaway gesture. 'You make it sound as if he's always cancelling dates. The design he was working on probably wasn't finished. He has deadlines to meet. He has to make up the time. Even at the weekend,' she added.

Laura was silent for a moment. She looked at Emily, holding her gaze, giving her a long look that said more than words ever could.

'All right, he does do it rather a lot,' Emily conceded. 'But that's only because he's taken on so much work and the freelancers he uses have either got other jobs on or they're off on holiday.'

Did she really believe that? She'd thought she did, but now....

Her friend's wide eyed gaze expressed the same doubts that were flitting across Emily's brain like bats in a night sky.

Laura wasn't finished. 'While we're on the subject, didn't Ethan promise you a holiday? Weren't the two of you off to Lake Maggiore?'

Emily all but flinched. She and Ethan had talked about going to Italy, it was true, but that was a while ago and there'd been no movement since. She wished she hadn't mentioned it to Laura now. But they were friends. Why wouldn't she have said anything?

'Sorry, Em,' Laura said, seeing Emily's face. 'I shouldn't have brought that up. Forget it. Here, have some more wine.' She picked up the bottle and tipped the dregs into Emily's glass.

'It's fine.' Emily sipped her drink, thankful that she'd had the forethought to walk here instead of driving. 'You can say anything you like. I'll let you know if you cross the line.' She winked.

'I'm concerned for you, that's all. Aside from Ethan, you've not had a serious relationship since the divorce and you deserve to find love again.'

Emily dissolved into giggles.

'Okay, that was cheesy,' Laura said, laughing too. 'You know what I mean, though. I wish you could find someone who truly makes you happy and if you ask me, Ethan's not making a very good job of it.'

Laura was as honest as a good friend should be, and Emily loved her for it. She deserved honesty in return – if only she could understand where her true feelings lay.

She sighed. 'It feels like failure, like there's something I should be doing, something everyone else knows but me, like a secret I've not been let in on. Why does it keep on happening? Why do I *make* it happen? Because it *is* me. It's my fault my relationships never work out. It has to be.'

She brought both hands down, heavily, on the broad arms of the chair as if to drive her point home – to herself as much as to Laura. She suddenly felt deathly tired, as if her little speech, unplanned, coming out of nowhere, had drained away all her energy.

'Em, *don't*.' Laura leaned in from her seat on the sofa. 'You know that's not true and you don't me to spell out why it's not. Anyway, it's not over with Ethan, is it? He may very well turn out to be *the one*. You love him, don't you? Maybe you two just need to talk.'

Emily sighed. 'I know. Of course I love him. I'm just having a moment, that's all. It's one hell of a coincidence, though, isn't it? One failed marriage and a string of bad relationships, or relationships that started well and went down the drain. I'm the common denominator, Laura. You can see that, surely?'

Laura shook her head firmly. 'Okay, your marriage didn't last the course but Mitch wanted out as much as you did, you know that. You did nothing wrong. You'd stopped making one another happy, ages before you actually split.'

'You're right. I've got no regrets there, not for marrying Mitch in the first place, nor for the way it ended. We were much happier apart, both of us,' Emily said truthfully.

She let a beat of silence fall, then, 'I never told you this before...'

'What didn't you tell me?' Laura's voice was warm with concern. She was such a good friend, it seemed wrong to keep secrets from her.

'I never told you what really triggered the split from Mitch. You only got the expurgated version. Truth to tell, I was ashamed. Oh, I'm not now. I've forgiven myself, and him. It was all so long ago...' She tailed off, not wanting to say the words out loud. But Laura wouldn't judge. 'I had an affair, well, more of a fling, really. Not that it makes it any better.'

'*Did you*?' Laura was plainly surprised.

'It didn't last long. I didn't want it to. He was engaged to someone else. We both regretted it almost as soon as it started.'

'Mitch found out?'

'Kind of. He guessed there was someone. I probably didn't hide it that well; we were so far apart, emotionally, by then. And then he confessed he'd done the same thing, slept with a woman he'd been friends with practically his whole life.' Emily gave a little laugh. 'Always a mistake, as he soon realised. So, we'd both misbehaved and that's when we knew we'd reached the end. Not because we couldn't have got past it, but because neither of us cared enough to try.' She folded her hands in her lap. 'So, that's me. I'm not that wonderful.'

'Is anybody? Honestly, you expect too much of yourself,' Laura said.

'Maybe if I'd tried harder with Mitch, and the boyfriends I've had since, things might have been different...'

'Em, this isn't like you. Where's it all coming from?'

'Haven't the faintest,' Emily said gloomily. Then a smile broke. 'Anyway, you started it.'

'I did, didn't I.' Laura clapped a hand to her forehead. 'Sorry.'

'No, *I'm* sorry. I'm not exactly the best company tonight, am I?' She put down the empty glass she'd been clutching as if it was a lifeline and smiled. 'That's it. Misery-fest over. I wouldn't mind a coffee if you're offering. My legs need recharging if I'm walking home.'

Laura went to the kitchen to make the coffee. Emily leaned back in her chair. She did love Ethan – she was in love with him. That much was true. But it wasn't hard to see where Laura's doubts, and her own, were coming from.

Take last night. She'd been so looking forward to Ethan arriving, telling her how lovely she looked in her new dress. Most likely, they'd have left his car at her house and taken a taxi to the restaurant. And another back again, and then...

Emily sighed. Laura was right. Ethan did let her down too often and she always rationalised it, made excuses for him. He hadn't met her parents yet; that was another thing. They lived in Brighton, only a few miles away, so there was no reason it hadn't happened, and the invitation was always on the table. But he'd always fought shy. Emily's mother thought it was strange and made no secret of it.

Laura was back with the coffee, her thoughts clearly still on Emily's love life.

'I've just remembered that dentist you went out with for a while – Ed, wasn't it? – now he was decent. Shy guy, didn't have a lot to say for himself, but I liked him. Clayton did, too. He thought he'd be good for you.'

Clayton was Laura's husband, her second; Laura had been widowed, sadly early.

'Ha!' Emily grinned. 'Good for me, as in keeping me in order, yes?'

Laura laughed. 'Something like that. No, he meant Ed would have looked after you. Clayton's a good judge of character.'

Emily gave her a wry look. 'Being looked after isn't always enough, though, is it?'

'Definitely not,' Laura said, lifting her eyes. 'Okay, point taken.'

'I got bored with Ed. He was too old, anyway.'

'Em, I meant what I said about talking to Ethan properly,' Laura said, after a pause. 'Tell him how you feel, really. It's no good glossing over the truth, is it?'

'Yep. I'll try. But when we're together, it's good, you know? And then I forget about all the times he's let me down and just have fun. There's nothing wrong with that.'

'Of course not. But if it's not going anywhere, then...?'

Laura didn't need an answer. They both knew what it would be – or should be.

Being here with her friend, talking things through, had shone a light on her deepest feelings about Ethan. What she was going to do about them eluded her, for now. Supposing they did sit down and talk properly, as Laura advised? Ethan might take exception, feel she was crowding him, pressurising him, any of that, which she would never mean to do. But any questioning on her side, any hint of her doubts about him, might come across that way. And then, he'd end it, and she'd be alone, again.

Laura got up and switched on the two enormous blue-and-white china lamps. Pools of lemony light spilled across the room. Emily hadn't noticed how dark it had become. She got up from the chair.

'It's late. I should be going.'

'Not that late. Clayton's not home yet. Stay, if you like. We could watch a film.'

'No. I've got work tomorrow and it's a school night for you.' Laura taught children with special educational needs at a school outside the village.

'Thanks for tonight,' Emily said, as they stood on the doorstep.

'It was only leftover lasagne.'

'No, I mean, for the little pep talk.'

'Any time.' Laura kissed Emily's cheek. 'Go straight home now. No talking to strangers.'

'Fat chance.'

CHAPTER 8

'Oh! Ramona. Hello.'

Emily's mind had been elsewhere. She'd forgotten about the girl from the library. But here she was at half past four on Wednesday, standing on the doorstep of Cloud Cottage, looking not the least bit shy, as she might have done to be knocking on the door of a virtual stranger.

'Hello, Emily,' she said. 'I've brought your money and my mother says thank you very much for lending it to me... her.'

Unzipping a black shoulder bag, she began rifling awkwardly in its depths. Emily could hear the clinking of coins.

'Come in for a minute.' Emily held the door ajar.

She led the way to the kitchen. Ramona put the bag on the counter top, fished inside again and the coins began to emerge, a handful at a time.

'That's one pound ninety,' she said, pointing at the little heap of cash, all in ten and twenty-pence pieces. 'Would you like to count it?'

'No, I'm sure it's correct,' Emily said, hiding a smile. 'Thank you. Did you have far to walk?'

Ramona looked puzzled for a moment. 'Oh. No. Not far. I really like your house. It's very pretty.'

'It is, isn't it? I'm glad you like it.'

'I do. I've seen it before. Just the outside of it.'

Ramona seemed to be in no hurry to leave. She stood against the kitchen counter, one foot crossed behind the other, looking thoughtful.

'Do you like reading, like your mum?' Emily asked.

Ramona seemed to be considering this.

'I do quite like it, but not as much as she does, and not the books we do in English Lit at school. At least, not all of them. I like writing more than reading.'

'Oh, really? What kind of writing do you do?'

'Essays at school, for English and history, and sometimes RE.' The girl looked at Emily as if the answer was obvious.

'Well, I expect you get good marks for those if it's something you enjoy.'

Ramona nodded absently. Emily gained the impression there was something on her mind other than small talk about reading and writing.

'I get good marks when I've had plenty of peace and quiet to write them in. But mostly it's not like that.'

'You mean it's not always quiet enough at home when you're doing your homework?' Emily said carefully, not wanting to openly criticise Ramona's living arrangements.

'Hardly *ever*. I've got a sister who's younger than me – I'm twelve, she's nine. I have to share a bedroom with her and she can be a real pest, sometimes. And I've got four older brothers. They're always fighting and stuff.' Ramona lifted her chin and gave Emily a direct look that seemed almost like a challenge. 'You try living with that lot in one small house with my mum and dad and a guinea-pig. The guinea pig's in a hutch in the garden, by the way, but the rest of us are in the house.'

'My, that is a houseful,' Emily said. 'I can imagine how noisy it is when everyone's at home.'

'Oh, it is. It's a nightmare of noise. I can't hear myself think most of the time.' Ramona's grey eyes lit up as she warmed to her theme. 'My dad says the boys sound like they've got hobnail boots on, the way they clump about.' She paused. 'Actually, what are hobnail boots?' She didn't wait for an answer. 'The boys are always scrapping, like I said. And the telly's on, like, *all* the time. The radio in the kitchen as well, when Mum's cooking.'

'Goodness. It's a wonder your mum manages to read at all, let alone take four books out of the library at one go.'

'Four...? Oh, yes, she gets them to save time.' The girl glanced down at her feet. 'Mum reads in the bath. With the door shut. It's the only place she can.'

Emily had a vision of an adult version of Ramona, up to her chest in bubbles, holding a library book. She wondered wildly if any of the books had been dropped in the bath water. Emily wasn't used to the company of young girls, but she'd associated with enough to know that this one wasn't your ordinary pre-teen. She was a breath of fresh air, and Emily liked that.

'Would you like a drink, Ramona? Some orange juice, perhaps, or cranberry? Or I have some cans of Coke, if you're allowed?'

'Are you having a drink?'

'I'm having a cup of tea. I usually have one when I get in from work.'

'Could I have tea, then?'

'Yes, of course. There might even be some cake left from the weekend.'

Of course there was. She always stocked up on everything for Ethan, although at this moment she couldn't think why she bothered.

Emily and Ramona sat one each end of the kitchen table, a

pot of tea and three-quarters of a chocolate gateau between them.

'My gra... mum makes lovely cakes.' Ramona said, nibbling delicately at her slice of cake. 'They're not as good as this, though.'

'I didn't make it. It came from the shop.'

'The village shop?'

'No, from a bakery in Cliffhaven.'

'Me and my friend Lilah go to Cliffhaven on the bus sometimes. On Saturdays, mostly. Were you there shopping?'

'I work there. I'm a journalist for the *Cliffhaven News*. That means I report on local events and write them up for the paper. The actual paper, and the online version.'

'I know what a journalist is.'

'Of course you do, sorry.'

'That's okay.' Ramona gave a smile that lit up her rather solemn little face.

Ramona licked a bit of chocolate icing from her fingertip. 'I'm going to be an archaeologist, or a palaeontologist. Probably an archaeologist because I want to discover a hidden city. That's why I need to do well at school. Would you like to see my collection of animal bones? I find them up on the Downs and in the fields around our house. I could bring them to show you, if you like? My favourite is the sheep's jawbone. It's still got most of the teeth.'

'Has it? Wow,' Emily said. 'What an exciting ambition. I'm sure you'll make an excellent archaeologist. I'll pass on the animal bones, though, if you don't mind.'

'You can't be sure I'll make an excellent archaeologist. Nobody can, because it's in the future.'

Emily wanted to smile, but she held it back in case Ramona thought she was making fun of her. 'Good point.'

The girl was on her second slice of cake. She'd accepted it

politely, and with thanks, and ate fast. She seemed hungry. She hadn't drunk much of her tea, though. It crossed Emily's mind that she'd only asked for tea because Emily was having it.

She watched Ramona surreptitiously over the top of her mug. She seemed small for her age, with delicate features that gave her an elfin appearance. Her straight, mid-brown hair was just above shoulder level with an overgrown fringe. It looked slightly in need of a wash, or at least a good brush. Emily's heart went out to her. An idea took root in her mind; a daft one, probably, but the girl could only say no. Before she could think much more about it, Emily heard herself suggesting to Ramona that she come here, to Cloud Cottage, to do her homework. Not every day, but on the days Emily worked at home or was planning to be back by the time school was out.

'You don't know me,' was the girl's first response. 'Why would you want to do that?'

'Because,' Emily said, 'I may not know you, but I can tell you want to get on in life and you have determination, and I admire that.' She was going to add 'especially in somebody as young as you', but that would sound patronising – if she hadn't already inadvertently crossed that line.

'Oh,' Ramona said, her eyes wide with astonishment. 'You'd really let me come here to your lovely cottage and study? That would be... brilliant! Thank you!'

'It wouldn't be every day, as I said. And not without your mum and dad's permission, obviously. I'd need to speak to them first.'

'Yes, all right.' Her face fell, then brightened almost instantly. 'Cool. I can arrange that, no problem. Mum wants me to get good grades. She'll be over the moon!'

Emily doubted Ramona's mother would go that far. From the sound of it, she didn't have time to draw breath, never mind get excited about her daughter having a quiet few hours to do her homework.

'Do you want to give me your mum's phone number before you go?'

Ramona was thoughtful, screwing her forehead up and narrowing her eyes. Eventually she said, 'I think I should tell her first. I mean, she knows I'm here today because she gave me the library money to give you, but I think it would be best coming from me in the first place.'

An old head on young shoulders, Emily thought. And yet, in other ways she seemed remarkably innocent and childlike.

'Okay, well I'll give you my phone number and your mum can ring me if she wants to, or you can ring me yourself and let me know what she said. Then, if it's a yes, we can arrange your first visit. Would that work?'

'Yes, it would.' Ramona got up from the chair, and came round to stand beside Emily, her arms by her sides. For one moment, Emily thought she was going to curtsey. 'Thank you very much for the tea and cake. I'll be going now.'

It wasn't until Ramona had left that Emily remembered Ethan was coming to dinner. He'd sent her a text this morning offering to take her out tonight to make up for cancelling on Sunday. Okay, fine, Emily had thought. And then, she'd thought again. She could get all dressed up tonight, only for him to let her down again; nothing would surprise her. She'd replied to say she'd love to see him but to come to the cottage and she'd cook. Minimal risk there. She had chicken and fish in the fridge – one of those would do. A simple supper and a cosy evening was much more in line with her mood than heading out to a restaurant.

The reason she'd been at the library yesterday was because

there were moves to close several of the smaller branch libraries in the area, of which Charnley Acre's was one. It was only open three days a week and alternate Saturday mornings, and was well-used at those times. The mobile library, calling one afternoon a week, was hardly an adequate replacement, and Emily had successfully pitched an article on the issue to her editor. She wouldn't have minded making a start on it tonight instead of entertaining Ethan. She thought about Ramona's overworked mother locking herself in the bathroom to grab a moment's peace to read her library book. She had no idea of the family's circumstances, of course, but they may not be able to afford to buy many books. In that case, the library would be essential, which was one of the points Emily intended to put forward in her article. Actually, when she spoke to Ramona's mother, she could mention the library proposal. As a regular user, the woman might be willing to give her a quote.

Emily's mind was still on the library matter as well as on Ramona and her intended visits to Cloud Cottage when Ethan gave his perfunctory knuckle tap on the back door and walked into the kitchen.

'Hey, you're early!' It was only six-thirty; she'd not been expecting him for another hour at least.

'Not caught you *in flagrante*, have I?' Ethan flung open the door of the larder and peered inside. 'Come out, come out, whoever you are!'

'Don't be daft.' Laughing, Emily stepped close to Ethan, her fingers raking his almost jet-black hair as she pulled him in for a kiss, her mood already lifting.

'Mmm, that's more like it.' His arms encircled her waist, pulling her closer. Lifting her shirt, he ran his hands up and down her bare back as they kissed again.

'I haven't changed yet,' she said, when they broke apart. 'And the dinner's not even started. I'm glad you're here, though.'

That was true. Her earlier distractions had dwindled, then melted away entirely at Ethan's touch. She loved this man, she really did, despite his flaws. Didn't she have just as many herself?

Ethan's arms stayed around her as he walked her backwards to the wall where he kissed her again, deeply, insistently.

She laughed softly when, eventually, the kissing stopped. 'You must be hungry. You've been at work all day. I was going to do something with chicken fillets, or there's fish, but I've just remembered I've got a pizza in the freezer. We could have it with salad and garlic bread?' Even simpler.

'Great.' Ethan's almost jet-black hair was standing on end where her hands had swept through it. 'But first things first.'

He hadn't even stayed for dinner. Upstairs in her bedroom, the outside world had receded as Emily lost herself in their lovemaking. And then, as they lay on their backs in the afterglow of sex, fingers entwined, he'd rolled way from her and said he was sorry but he had to go.

He hadn't sounded sorry. He'd given her the most perfunctory of explanations – no explanation at all, really, she realised as she heard the front door close on Ethan and the growl of the engine as he drove away. He'd said something vague about a new contract and a meeting he'd forgotten all about until now.

Work. It was always about work with Ethan. Listening to him, you'd have thought there was nothing else going on in his life other than his graphic design business, and Emily. And in her estimation, those two things featured eighty-twenty – if she featured at all.

She flapped the duvet back across the bed. She felt sad, disappointed, almost to the point of tears. How fast everything changed, and changed again in a matter of hours! She wondered what Laura would make of all this. Actually, she didn't need to wonder; her friend's careful words of caution still echoed in her brain.

She showered and changed into a pair of comfy joggers and a fresh T-shirt, looping her sky blue cashmere cardigan around her shoulders, more for the comfort than the warmth. Back in the kitchen, she took the pizza out of the freezer, stared at it for a moment, then put it back again. She wasn't at all hungry now. She'd have something later.

She made a mug of tea and took it through to the living room. She could make a start on the library article – she had enough information to be going on with – but one look at her laptop on the table told her she wasn't in the mood for work. She left it where it was and settled down on the sofa to watch TV but concentration evaded her. She felt twitchy and restless as a procession of unwanted thoughts invaded her mind and refused to be quelled.

At half-past nine, unable to stand it any longer, she grabbed her mobile and rang Ethan's number. It went straight to voicemail. She didn't leave a message. Five minutes later, he rang her back, sounding strangely out of breath.

'Hi, Em. I saw you'd called.'

'I did. Are you okay? Only you sound as if you've run up a flight of stairs.' She kept her voice deliberately light. She had plenty to say to him, not all of which he would like, but this wasn't the time.

'Of course I'm okay. I was in the middle of something when you rang.'

'Nothing too important, I hope.' She wasn't going to apologise for disturbing him, not after he'd effectively run out on her. 'Anyway, how did your meeting go?'

'What? Oh, yes, fine. It's all good.'

'You sorted out the new contract?'

'Yep, all done and dusted.'

'Funny time of day for a business meeting. Or week, for that matter.' She regretted her words with their implied criticism immediately but failed to save them in time.

'Not everybody works nine-to-five, Monday to Friday, Emily.' She heard the annoyance in his tone. Well, too bad.

'Yes, Ethan, I do know. I work for a newspaper, remember? My hours aren't always convenient either.'

'No.'

Silence. Ethan seemed lost for words. Emily, on the other hand, was building up a vast store of them. This wasn't how she'd intended to play it. She'd intended simply to ask if all was well with him, say sorry he'd had to miss dinner, but she'd cook him something really special, not pizza, on whatever night he was free. His reaction – his sharpness when all she'd done was ask after his welfare – put paid to that.

'Actually, you did me a favour,' she said, her tone less than friendly. 'I'm working on a potentially thorny article and I could use the time to prepare.' He didn't need to know she had no intention of writing a word of it tonight.

'Ah, well, it worked out for the best then.'

Just that. He didn't ask what the article was about, or express regret that they hadn't been able to spend the evening together as planned. Defeated, Emily was about to say goodnight and end the call when Ethan, typically, said something that went halfway towards redeeming himself.

He spoke in lowered tones, so that she had to listen hard to hear. 'You're an amazing, sexy woman, you know that? I've been thinking about what we did earlier, ever since I left.'

'You're not so bad yourself.' The smile came unbidden to her lips as she thought about the rumpled bed upstairs, the pillows on the floor.

'I love you, Em. I'll see you soon,' Ethan said. 'We'll go out to dinner, somewhere special.'

'Okay. And then we can talk about Lake Maggiore again, see if we can pin down some dates. I'm owed some time off.'

A pause, then, 'Yes, sure.'

He was gone. Emily looked at the clock. It was still only a quarter to ten, probably too late for Ethan to drive back here from Brighton. She tried not to think that it wouldn't have hurt him to make the effort. But perhaps he'd had a drink with his client. And in any case, he'd only have had to get up early and drive back again.

And there she went again, making excuses for him.

Something had to change; she'd known that, deep down, for a while now. But wasn't compromise an essential part of a loving relationship? Nobody was perfect, least of all her. Perhaps she expected too much.

CHAPTER 9

'Show me some of your writing. Where's your poetry analysis, the Robert Frost thing we're handing in this afternoon?'

Without waiting for Lilah's response, Ramona bent down and pulled her friend's English file out of her schoolbag where she'd dropped it on the floor beside her chair and opened it out on the table.

The buzz and clatter of the school refectory at lunch break went on around them, accompanied by the mixed smells of fried chips, cabbage and Cornish pasties.

'What're you doing? What d'you want that for?' Lilah looked across while Ramona leafed through the file but didn't try to grab it back.

'Yep, not bad, not bad at all. This'll do.' Ramona shuffled closer to Lilah so they were elbow to elbow and looked Lilah in the eye.

'I know that look,' Lilah said. 'Not to do with homework, is it? You've done yours, I bet. You don't need to copy mine. Like you ever would, clever clogs.'

'I don't. It's not that. It's... I need a favour, a biggish one. Please don't say no. It's dead important.'

'You don't have to beg. I'll do it, whatever it is,' Lilah said, craftily securing the favour she wanted from Ramona, which was to give her an alibi should she ever, *ever*, be asked out by Jamie. 'What's it got to do with English homework, though?'

'It's not the homework itself, it's the writing. I'm just checking how it looks.' Lilah was known for changing her writing style all the time. Her latest assignment, luckily, was written neatly and tidily, not too many loops and swirls. It looked suitably businesslike. 'All you have to do is copy what I've written in the same writing as you've done here. On this pad.'

Ramona pushed across a small pad of paper. It was Tilly's best notepaper, pale blue, kept for best, even though she hardly ever wrote letters any more. She opened the pad at the first sheet, slid another piece of paper with her own writing next to it and tapped it with her finger. 'There.'

'Copy it exactly?' Lilah said.

'That's what copy means. You don't have to say exactly.'

Lilah raised her eyes. 'Give us a pen, then.'

'Can you use yours, your best one?'

'It's the same as yours. What's the difference?'

'It's yours, not mine.' Wasn't it obvious, the difference? Nobody else would know, but she would.

Lilah fished in her bag, found her pen and cast her eyes across the paper with Ramona's writing on it. She frowned.

'That's the easy part, the copying,' Ramona said hurriedly. 'The second part of the favour is much bigger.'

'Is it?'

'Yes, *much* bigger.'

'Go on then. Tell me the worst.'

Ramona took a deep breath. This had to work; she was relying on Lilah's complete co-operation, which *should* be okay, but you never knew with Lilah. 'Right, well…you can't ask me any questions about this and when you've written it, you have to forget all about it and never think about what you wrote or tell anybody you wrote it.'

'How can I not think about it? I can't control what I think about, can I?'

'Actually, you can, if you really concentrate.'

'Oh *God*.' Lilah shook her head at the apparent craziness of all this. But she took up the pen and began to write.

She seemed to take an age. But at least she was being careful with her writing. Eventually, she finished, and pushed the pad back to Ramona.

'There. That do?'

'Perfect. There's just one more thing.' Ramona produced a matching blue envelope. 'Can you write *Emily* on the front of this?' She wished she'd thought to ask for her last name. It would have added a useful touch of formality.

Lilah did as she was asked.

'Thank you,' Ramona said.

The envelope had lost its stickiness, and no matter how much she licked it, the glue wasn't gluey any more. Never mind, she could put a bit of Sellotape across it when she got home.

She didn't *quite* trust Lilah not to ask her any questions later – she knew she would have done if it had been the other way around – but Jamie and his mates had got up from the table two rows away from them and were heading for the door, pulling Lilah's attention right away from the note she'd written, and everything else in the world.

Ramona pushed back her chair and stood up. 'I'm going to the library. See you later.'

'Yeah, laters,' Lilah said vaguely, her eyes glued to Jamie's back.

Ramona's stomach turned over as Emily peeled the Sellotape off the envelope, slipped the note out and began to read. She read silently, but moving her lips so that Ramona was able to follow and say the words herself, inside her head:

Dear Emily, it was very kind of you to invite my eldest daughter, Ramona, to Cloud Cottage where you live. I understand it is very quiet there and that is just what Ramona needs if she is going to pass all her exams, go to university, and become an archaeologist. I hereby give my permission for Ramona to do her homework at your house as and when it is convenient for yourself.

When Emily got to the end part, she read it aloud, but softly.

'Thank you very much. Yours sincerely, Mrs Donnelly.' Emily looked over at Ramona, who was sitting on Emily's sofa in her cosy, colourful living room. 'What's your mother's first name?'

Ramona's brain scraped around for Lilah's mother's name. Eventually it came to her: 'Sharon.' She couldn't say Tilly, or Matilda, could she? That would have given the game away.

'So, you're Ramona Donnelly?'

'Yes.' Ramona released the breath she'd been holding. She nodded firmly. 'I am.'

At least she'd told one piece of truth since she got here. Not that it made up for the rest. If there was any way other than to tell a pack of lies... But this was the best idea she'd come up with. The *only* idea, but a good one, she thought. Emily was kind and friendly, as well as very pretty for an oldish person. She shouldn't be told lies. It couldn't be helped, though. Tilly would approve, if she knew. She was a private person; she wouldn't like to think of her business being made public to all and sundry. This way, Ramona was protecting Tilly's privacy as well as safeguarding her own precarious living situation.

Ramona watched her new friend carefully for signs of doubt. She needed Emily. Despite her self-assertion that she could manage perfectly well alone until Tilly came home, it was becoming clear that having a reliable adult to hand made her feel better about it, as well as safer.

Emily appeared to be thinking hard, her eyes on the note in her hand. Eventually, she looked at Ramona and smiled. 'Well, I'd liked to have spoken to your mother but I suppose this will do for now.' She put the note down on the coffee table.

'She'd liked to have spoken to you, too, but she's very busy right now. *Very* busy.'

'Yes, I imagine she is. Where do you live, Ramona?'

Ramona hesitated for only a second while her brain rapidly formed an acceptable reply. 'The other side of Charnley Acre.' She pointed vaguely, in no particular direction.

'Where, exactly?'

Ramona ran a virtual map of the village through her mind, very fast. 'Meadowside.'

'That's the little estate just off the main road to Cliffhaven, isn't it?'

'Yes, that's it.'

Ramona felt hot and uncomfortable. She'd had to give Emily a Charnley Acre address; Lilah's family lived in a different village, which wouldn't have worked at all. Any more questions like that and her powers of invention might let her down. Perhaps she should write everything down, the lies she'd told Emily, and the true bits, in case she forgot what she'd said.

For a little while, nobody spoke. Ramona heard the soft ticking of the clock, and the birds tweeting in the garden. It reminded her of life at Number One The Pasture, before it happened. Although it was only seven days, one hour and fifteen minutes since she'd come home and found Tilly missing, it felt like a century. A trickle of sadness ran down inside her and pooled at the pit of her stomach.

She'd phoned the hospital again before she'd set out for Cloud Cottage. A different nurse had answered, which was a good thing. A man. He'd sounded in too much of a hurry to ask who was speaking. Mrs Donnelly had rallied, he told her, but was very weak and was being kept under observation. In her most grown-up voice, Ramona thanked him for the information, and for looking after Till... Mrs Donnelly so well, but before she'd got to the end of this speech, the phone had gone dead.

After she'd made the phone call, Ramona had crossed herself. She wasn't a Catholic; in fact, she didn't believe in God at all – where was the *evidence*? – but it had seemed a fitting way to show how thankful she was that Tilly was all right, even though there was nobody to see.

She glanced across at the table on the far side of the room where she'd put her school bag.

'I must let you get on with your homework,' Emily said, noticing. 'It's what you're here for, after all. Would you like some orange squash and a biscuit before you start?'

Ramona said she would, please, and Emily got up from her chair then turned back to Ramona, looking thoughtful.

'Ramona, may I ask you one more question?'

Now what? 'Yes?'

'Are you by any chance related to anybody else in the village called Donnelly? A lady called Matilda, perhaps?'

Ramona swallowed hard, screwing up her forehead in the deepest frown she had. 'I don't know anyone called that. Why?'

'It doesn't matter. Donnelly's not that unusual a name. I only wondered if there was any connection.' Emily smiled. 'I'll get your drink.' And off she went to the kitchen.

The following morning, Saturday, Ramona noticed that the water coming out of the shower wasn't as hot as usual. The shower was on the wall over the bath; Tilly had had it put in, the year before last. Ramona had chosen the curtain for it from a catalogue. It was red, white, and blue, with a cheerful seaside theme. She fiddled with the settings on the dial of the shower, but nothing happened except the water got a little bit colder instead of warmer. But it was a warm day, so it didn't matter.

It mattered more that the washing machine didn't seem to be spinning the clothes properly. The washing machine was much older than the shower. Last night, she'd taken her things out to find them in a much soggier state than usual. She'd taken a chance that it wouldn't rain overnight and had hung them out to drip-dry on the line which ran from a hook on the wall of the cottage to a handy tree. It hadn't rained, but when she went outside in her pyjamas this morning to check on the washing, she'd found it was still quite wet.

Ramona had glanced up at the sky, which was pure blue all over. The sun would dry the washing, and the washing machine would sort itself out – that's what Tilly would say.

Even so, these setbacks reminded Ramona that she needed to be extra careful with the money, so that there'd be enough left for Tilly to get the shower and the washing machine mended when she came home, if necessary. The bank account balance didn't seem quite so reassuring as it had before.

But she still needed cash for groceries and after breakfast she walked to the village, used the cashpoint in the post office and bought what she needed from the shop, keeping her purchases to the bare minimum.

Coming out of the shop with her two full carrier bags, she thought she could run to an iced bun from the bakery across the road. She'd bought a small bag of cheap flour and half a dozen eggs, intending to make fairy cakes for tomorrow – Sunday tea wasn't 'proper' without cakes – but an iced bun would be a treat for today. Inside the bakery, the smell of dough, sugar and fresh bread made her mouth water. She'd buy two buns, she could afford that; she hadn't been extravagant with her other food shopping. She'd get one to have straight away and one for later – or, one for her grandmother, should the hospital pop her back home later, which was always a possibility.

As she joined the queue in the bakery, she saw a felt-tipped notice taped to the glass shelf covering the cakes: *Saturday staff wanted*.

'Could I apply for the job?' Ramona asked, as she reached the front of the queue and paid for her buns. 'I'm looking for a Saturday job. I'm very willing.'

The man serving eyed her across the counter. Ramona smoothed her hair back and pulled herself up to her full height.

'How old are you?'

'Twelve, but I'm very mature for my age.'

'Ah, sorry, love. Thirteen's the bottom line, it's the law, and even then there's rules about hours of work in school term time, and all that.'

Ramona nodded. It was what she'd expected – she knew the minimum employment age, everybody did – but it had been worth a try. It was only a village bakery, after all. She could serve bread and cakes standing on her head. Come to think of it, perhaps she should have thrown that in as an extra talent. If Lilah had been here, they'd have giggled like anything about that.

Instead, Ramona left the bakery feeling slightly offended.

The Ginger Cat café was nearby. Bolder now, she went in and asked if they needed any help on a Saturday. The couple who ran the café, Jo and Lloyd, were kind, friendly people. Everybody in the village knew them, even if they didn't know everybody. Hopefully, they didn't know Ramona.

'You don't look thirteen,' Lloyd said, giving her a long look. 'That's the age you have to be. In any case, we weren't thinking of taking anyone else on at the moment.'

'I will be thirteen in four months and two days. That's not so long to wait, is it? I'll do the washing up or clean the floor, or anything. Nobody would know.'

Lloyd smiled, not unkindly. 'Sorry, sweetheart, it's a no-can-do.'

'Okay. Thank you anyway.' Ramona smiled back. It wasn't his fault, was it?

Now that she'd had some practice, it was worth one more try, surely? Back on the other side of the high street, she went into the hairdressers and offered to sweep up hair, clean basins, anything they wanted.

'I'm hardworking and very cheap,' she said.

The woman she was speaking to, the one with a name badge saying *Kirsty*, who seemed be in charge, had a big grin on her face. Other people laughed softly, like they knew they shouldn't be laughing. Honestly, what did a girl have to do to be taken seriously around here, let alone get an honest day's work?

'I'm sorry but you're not old enough yet. Come back when you're thirteen, actually make that fourteen. I don't take on that young,' Kirsty said, with a kind smile.

Ramona crossed the fingers of both hands, which wasn't easy with the shopping bags.

'I am thirteen. I'm over thirteen, nearly fourteen. I look young for my age.'

She'd told so many lies now, one more little white one wouldn't hurt.

'You'd have to bring in your birth certificate, you know, and a reference from your school.' Kirsty looked apologetic, as if she'd liked to have helped.

Defeated, Ramona looked at the floor. There was a lot of hair down there. It looked as if they could do with somebody to sweep it up. Obviously, it wasn't going to be her. Their loss.

'Bye, then,' she said, and sailed out of the door, her head held high.

Later, Ramona and Lilah went to the cinema in Cliffhaven, to the five o'clock showing. The film was an American high school comedy, not really Ramona's kind of thing but it was the only film on with a 12 rating, and it was quite funny. Afterwards, they had burgers and chips at McDonald's, which Lilah's dad had given them the money for. Every little helped, Ramona thought, as she scooped out the last of her fries from the paper bag and popped them into her mouth with greasy fingers.

'Shall we do something tomorrow?' Lilah asked, when they were on the bus home. 'I could come to yours if you like?'

Lilah hardly ever came to Ramona's house; it was more convenient, and more fun, for Ramona to go to hers. She was, Ramona suspected, making a concession there. Either that, or she felt like a bit of peace and quiet away from the noise and chaos of her own house.

Ramona felt her face heating up with sudden embarrassment. And yes, if she was honest, shame. Shame that the cottage had got into a bit of a state, even though she'd done her best to keep everything clean and tidy. Shame that she'd let her home-alone situation run on for so long, and kept it secret from her best friend – from everyone.

But it was too late now. She'd have to see it through, no matter what.

Her throat felt tight. She swallowed the feeling away. 'No, I can't, sorry. Tilly wants me to go and visit her friend with her. Her friend, Mary. She lives in Lewes. We'll do something next weekend, though.' Tilly would be home by then and life would return to normal.

'Okay. Text me anyway,' Lilah said, giving her a friendly nudge. 'See you Monday!'

She got off the bus at the next stop to change to the bus that would take her home. Ramona stayed on, feeling miserable as the bus jogged on towards Charnley Acre. The lies were building up. They lay in a great heap at the back of her mind, like the craggy lumps of black coal in the coal-store at the side of the cottage. But if she was to avoid being carted off by one of those social people to some institution to live with strangers, the heap would have to stay right where it was. It wouldn't be forever.

It was a mystery, though, that Tilly hadn't managed to phone her yet. But the nurse had said she was weak. And – Ramona didn't like to think about this, but the idea was there all the same – Tilly might have forgotten the phone number, or thought she'd already spoken to Ramona. Or, she'd got in a muddle with the days and didn't know how long she'd been away. When her head let her remember, she would ask to use the phone in the hospital, of course she would. Either that, or the ambulance would simply bring her home and they'd carry on as normal, and no more would be said about it.

Ramona woke up on Sunday morning to the familiar cooing of the wood pigeons in the trees behind the cottage . She wondered how she was going to fill the day. The housework was done, a bit sketchily but it was good enough. The garden had been watered with the metal can. She'd taken care of both things yesterday. She'd done all her homework at Emily's on Friday, apart from some reading – *Lord of the Flies*, for English – and she could do that in bed tonight. Reading at night helped her to fall asleep faster. She hadn't got used to being in bed and hearing no sound from the television downstairs, or Tilly moving about in the kitchen. It wasn't scary, hearing nothing but the creaking of the house, the occasional car passing on the road, and the owl's call. Not scary at all. Just... different.

The idea came to her as she was spreading butter on her toast. She knew exactly what she wanted to do today: she wanted to see Tilly. *Had* to see her, and never mind the consequences. There would be plenty of hospital visitors on a Sunday, too many for the nurses to take any notice of her and start asking questions. And even if they did, she could lie her way out of it. Goodness knows, she'd had enough practice. Tilly was hardly likely to waylay a nurse and say, *'This is my granddaughter and I've left her on her own at home.'* Time enough to deal with that if it happened.

Ramona caught the two o'clock bus to Cliffhaven. Before the bus got to the town centre, it looped around a small estate of newish houses, then doubled back and stopped right outside the main entrance to Cliffhaven General. Before she set out, she'd made up a posy of flowers from the garden – zinnias, pinks, and marigolds, tied together with sprigs of greenery, a plastic bag round the stems to keep them fresh. The bunch looked so pretty; she couldn't wait for Tilly to see them.

As she got off the bus, she realised this was the most scared she'd felt since it all began. She'd never known her grandmother in any situation other than at home, being ordinary, doing everyday things. Would seeing her in the hospital bed make her suddenly tearful, and would Tilly be upset, too? What would she do, how would she cope, if that happened? Now she was actually here, the likelihood of somebody catching on and realising Tilly had nobody in the world but her seemed all too real.

But it was too late now. She must stop thinking about herself. If she was scared, how must Tilly be feeling, abandoned in hospital, not able to get to a phone, wanting to go home but nobody would let her? Ramona took several deep breaths and joined the straggle of visitors and nurses in the corridor which smelt of rubber and the toilet cleaner they used at home.

Primrose Ward, that was the one. Pretty name. Ramona followed the signs, which led her to the end of a long, green painted corridor and up one flight of stairs. The doors to the ward stood open; other visitors stood about or sat in chairs beside the beds. Ramona scanned both sides of the ward. No Tilly. Two of the beds had curtains pulled round. If one of those contained her grandmother, that couldn't be a good sign. The empty bed at the end didn't help her nervousness either.

She was about to go to the first curtained bed and peep inside, when a woman in a green uniform stopped her and asked if she could help. The nurses seemed all to wear blue uniforms. Perhaps this person was less important and less likely to be difficult. Ramona took heart from that.

'I'm looking for Mrs Donnelly. Somebody... a friend, asked me to drop these flowers in to her. A friend who couldn't get here herself.'

Well, it didn't pay to take chances.

'I don't think...' the woman glanced around, frowning and cupping her chin. 'Wait there, I'll go and check for you.'

Ramona did as she was told and stood and waited. The flowers in her hand trembled a bit. A couple of petals detached themselves and drifted to the floor. Could Tilly be...? Ramona could hardly bear the thought that had entered her brain. But no, she mustn't think like that. Tilly was fine, or she would be, very soon.

The woman was back. 'You've just missed her, I'm afraid. Mrs Donnelly was moved this morning.'

'Oh.' The breath left Ramona's lungs all in a rush. 'Which ward is she in now, please?'

'Ah, no, lovey. She's left the hospital and been transferred to Seaview House. That's a nursing home a couple of miles from here. It's got a few NHS beds, and she has one of them. That's all I know, I'm afraid. If you want to know about her condition, you'll have to ask the staff nurse, although–' she looked Ramona up and down '–you seem rather young to be hearing the ins and outs.' She paused. 'Actually, dear, we don't allow flowers to be brought in, although those are very pretty.'

No flowers? What kind of a hospital was this?

Calmer now, her courage revived, Ramona stood up straight and looked the woman in the eye. 'Thank you very much for the information. I'll pass it on to Mrs Donnelly's friend. She can ring up the new place, can't she?'

The green-uniformed woman nodded. She looked doubtful, in the same sort of way Emily had. Why did everyone seem to have questions they weren't asking? Well, never mind. That was their problem, not hers.

Ramona turned on her heel and marched out of the ward, and away from the hospital. She caught the next bus home, still clutching the flowers.

CHAPTER 10

Tilly opens her eyes and the light hits her full in the face. A window, wide, high. She doesn't recognise anything in this room, or outside the window. Has she been here before?

'Am I at home?' She doesn't think she's home. Best to make sure, though.

'No, dear. This is Seaview House.'

What house? Where is she? Tilly reaches out, stretching her arm to its fullest extent. Her empty hand clutches at air.

'There, there. Nothing to get agitated about. The hospital sent you so we can look after you better. Remember the doctor telling you?'

Tilly's arm comes down again, like a foreign thing.

Her mind isn't clear – never is now – but clear enough.

'Nobody told me. They brought me in the...you know, the white thing...'

'The ambulance'.

'Yes, the ambulance. Nobody said where.'

'Didn't they? Oh well, never mind.'

A smile. Lipstick. Coral colour, like Tilly once wore. She

remembers the lipstick, and the pressed pink powder in a compact, and the mascara you spat on to make it work. She can't be so bad then, if she remembers that. Except her mind insists on chasing something – a thought, a memory, what? Tilly only knows she has to catch it. She knows it's very important that she does. She's been trying to tell them – tell *somebody* – but the moment the words start to sound right, off they race again, hiding themselves beneath a blanket of cotton wool inside her stupid head. *Come on, Tilly!*

'Tea's coming in a minute, and Madeira cake. It's always Madeira on a Sunday.'

The tea comes in a beaker with a lid, like a baby's. A man brings it on a trolley, with the yellow cake.

'I'd like a china cup, please.'

'Right you are. Have this for now and it'll be china next time.'

That's something, at any rate.

The woman has gone now. A nurse, was she, or a doctor? She never said. They don't, do they? The man with the trolley rattles off, too. He's whistling. The noise of it goes right through her. The pillows behind her head keep slipping down. Pillows, but she isn't in bed, and she isn't wearing a nightie. She's in trousers and some kind of pull-on top. Hers? There's a bed, over there, beside the window, but this is a chair they've put her in. There's somebody sitting in another chair across the other side of the room. She's not moving. Perhaps she's dead and nobody's noticed.

Tilly draws on her tea through the ridiculous spout. Has she had another one of her funny turns – her drop-downs, as she calls them? Is that why she's here? Has somebody found her and brought her here? She wishes she could remember. Nobody knows about the other times. The times when she's found herself on the floor. Out in the garden once, all the washing on top of her! This is it when you live alone. Nobody to see, nobody to ship you off to the doctor to be poked about. And boy, what a blessing that is. If anyone is in charge of their own destiny, it's Tilly.

Oh, what *is* it she's trying to get a grip on? Something's not right, she should be telling somebody, doing something... but what *is* it?

The nurse, or doctor, or whoever she is, comes back. She's brought some things. Soap and a flannel, a towel, and a little bowl.

'These are yours, Mrs Donnelly. I'll just slip them in this cupboard – see, here? Then if you don't fancy the bathroom at any time, you can do your hands and face. Somebody will bring the water. Is that all right?'

'Thank you.' Tilly smiles. Or thinks she does.

Of course it's not all right! Is she meant to have a wash here, in this room? She'll wait until she gets home, thank you very much. No point in upsetting anyone, though.

The name comes back into her head. 'Is Caroline coming to fetch me soon?'

'Mrs Donnelly, who is Caroline? Can you remember? You asked me before, but I don't know who she is.'

Tilly waves the empty beaker. 'Oh, don't worry about that, dear. I shall introduce you when she gets here.'

A laugh comes out of those coral lips. Has something funny happened?

'I can see you're going to be a real tonic, Mrs Donnelly. Tilly.'

'I shall do my best.' Tilly gives a little nod.

And then she's alone again. Apart from the person in the other chair, who might be dead, for all she knows.

CHAPTER 11

Seaview House – and, naturally, Tilly – were on Ramona's mind all the way on the bus to school on Monday, then all through double maths and PE. Now it was English, and her mind was swiftly diverted by Mr Roper, who was also her form teacher, asking her to read out loud a passage from *Lord of the Flies* then explain to the class what she thought it meant. No problem there. She'd read on through the book in bed last night, right past the place they'd got to in class; there wasn't much that was difficult about it, and at least they'd done with Jane Austen for the time being. Concentrating hard on the story had stopped her from noticing the silence in the house so much.

Mr Roper – known as Groper by most but not by Ramona, because she considered him an excellent teacher – moved on to somebody else, catapulting Ramona's thoughts right back to their starting place. Seaview House: she'd looked it up on the laptop as soon as she'd got home yesterday. She'd wondered if she should have asked at the hospital for directions and gone straight there, instead of jumping on the bus back to the village. But it might have been too far to walk. Besides, she'd used up all her courage going to the hospital in the first place. She'd needed to go home and have a good think about what she'd learned. It was disappointing that she'd missed Tilly, though. Her heart gave a little twinge every time she thought about her gran.

The nursing home looked pretty from the picture on the website. It wasn't huge, like the hospital. It was painted white, with a red tiled roof that went up and down in points, and thin chimneys, like a house in an old-fashioned children's book. There was a garden in front with a black railing, and lots of windows looking out to sea. It was on the main road that ran along beside the cliffs, which must make it very windy there in the winter. She hoped Tilly could see the sea from where she was. She would like that, even though she'd rather be looking at the hills behind Number One The Pasture.

When Ramona had finished reading about Seaview House, which hadn't taken long because there hadn't been much to read, she'd read about something called dementia. She'd heard the word, of course, and knew roughly what it meant. What she hadn't known was that there were lots of different kinds of dementia, depending on what the person had wrong with them and what had caused it. That had come as quite a surprise. She'd bookmarked the page so that she could read it again later.

One thing became crystal clear as she read, and that was that the hospital had made a big mistake. They'd muddled Tilly up with somebody else, and instead of sending her home, she'd ended up in a place for people who had this dementia thing, which Tilly most definitely did not have. She might have forgotten a few things recently, but she'd said that was because she was getting old. They'd laughed about it together.

Ramona might have been upset and angry about the mistake. She recognised the beginnings of those feelings in the pit of her stomach and in the prickles down her spine, but she pushed them away. Everyone she'd spoken to at the hospital on the phone and at Primrose Ward itself had been friendly and practical and helpful, even when they were dead busy. So, it stood to reason that one of those people would suddenly realise what had happened and send somebody back to Seaview House to collect Tilly and bring her home. It could be tomorrow, perhaps. Or even today! Wouldn't that be marvellous, for Tilly and her?

Ramona allowed herself to feel a teeny bit excited at this thought, but not too much, because she didn't know for sure what was going to happen. She could only imagine, and hope, and wait. Some days, she felt she'd been waiting all her life.

She turned down Lilah's invitation to go to her house after school and stay for dinner, even though she very much wanted to go. If Tilly came back this evening, she must be there. It would be horrible if she came home to an empty house, after all she'd been through. Also, Ramona would need to explain about the washing machine not spinning, and about the water – from all the taps now, not just the shower – going cold, before Tilly found out for herself. And she'd need to be told why there were lots of baked beans and tins of soup in the cupboard and not much else, apart from the fish and chicken in the freezer which would need proper cooking, but not until Tilly was up to it. There was cheese, bread and cereal – the eggs had run out – and a tub of cheap vanilla ice cream in the freezer. Ramona was fine on her limited diet, and she still had money for school lunch, but she had to be careful not to spend too much in case the money in the bank ran out.

Monday went, and Tuesday came, and Wednesday. Tilly didn't come. Ramona decided that if she didn't come home by the weekend, she would have to go to Seaview House. That would need more thinking about beforehand, even more than she'd done before she'd gone to the hospital, and perhaps her thinking would lead her to realise she couldn't go there at all.

She'd been living on her own for over two weeks now, which would give more reason for people to get all fussed up over.

Friday came round again, surprisingly quickly. Ramona went to Cloud Cottage after school. She still felt guilty about the stories she'd told Emily – okay, lies – but it felt even safer now to have an adult around, other than her teachers, even though she couldn't actually talk to her about Tilly and everything, and she had to be really careful not to say anything that would give her away.

She'd been going to Cloud Cottage almost every day after school. Emily was working on her library article, which meant she got to be at home a lot while she gathered all the information together. She'd told Ramona what it was all about, talking to her as if she was a grown-up and not a pre-teen. There'd been a tricky moment when Emily had asked her what sort of books her mother liked best, and whether she bought books as well as getting them from the library. But Ramona's mind automatically switched itself into the right zone with only the tiniest hesitation, and the answers came easily.

It was like living two lives – one real and the one she'd invented, which seemed very real indeed when she had to talk about it.

She'd been concentrating on her biology homework and hadn't heard the door open. When she glanced up, Emily was there, and she had a man with her. He looked about Emily's age, whatever that was, had broad shoulders, and lots of dark hair, even darker than Emily's. There was stubble on his chin, not in a scruffy way but like he meant it to be there. It suited him, made him look like somebody from film and TV whose name she couldn't quite remember.

'Ramona, this is Ethan,' Emily said. She gave the man a nudge, and he said 'hello' to Ramona. He didn't smile, though.

He'd said 'hello' out of the corner of his mouth, as if he'd rather not be saying it.

Ramona lifted her chin and said 'hello' back. She didn't smile either.

'Yes, well, we'll leave you to get on.' Emily hustled Ethan off to the kitchen and shut the door behind her.

She'd looked a bit awkward, Ramona thought, as if she didn't know what to do with herself. That wasn't like Emily. Ramona strained to listen to the conversation behind the door. She couldn't make out many of the actual words, but by the up-and-down tone of the voices – mostly up – she gathered there was some sort of argument going on. Perhaps she should pack up her homework and get out of the way.

No, that wasn't right. Why should she be the one to leave? She'd been invited to Cloud Cottage, the same as Ethan – if he had been invited and not just turned up.

Ramona stopped listening and carried on adding labels to her diagram of the human digestive system.

Not long after, Emily slipped quietly into the room and sat in the armchair with her laptop and her notes, which Ramona thought must be to do with the library thing she was working on.

She smiled as Ramona looked up from her work. 'How's it going?' She always asked that, which was nice.

'*Quite* well. The inside of a human being is very complicated.'

Emily smiled again, wider this time. 'It certainly is.'

'Except,' Ramona continued, scratching her nose, 'when it's the skeleton, because all the bones meet all the other bones and it's easy to remember where they all go, even the tiny ones.'

Emily laughed. 'I'm not sure I'd remember. I didn't do very well at that kind of thing at school.'

Ramona sighed. 'I've got to do well at *everything*. I can't afford to take any chances. That's what my... my mum says, anyway.' She took her lucky charm out of her pencil case and held it delicately between finger and thumb. 'Did I show you this? It's part of a mouse's skull. Or it could be a shrew's. It's not easy to tell as they're quite similar.'

'Yes, you showed me the other day. Very nice.'

Emily's face said she didn't think it was nice at all but was being polite.

Ramona decided to change the subject. Besides, she couldn't help being a little bit curious. 'Has your friend gone now?'

'Ethan? Yes, he's gone.'

Ramona thought about the argument she'd overheard but decided not to mention it. It was none of her business, was it?

'He didn't stay long, did he?'

'Nope.'

'Oh well, I expect he was in a hurry,' Ramona said.

She tucked the lucky skull back inside her pencil case and concentrated on the diagram. When she looked up again, Emily had gone from the room, leaving her laptop behind.

CHAPTER 12

*I*f Ethan thought she was going to be ready and waiting any time he deigned to put in an appearance, he had another think coming.

Spontaneity enhanced a relationship, kept the romance going, and that was fine. Emily had been delighted to see him yesterday, her plans to catch up with some work willingly set aside the moment he'd pitched up at Cloud Cottage unannounced. He'd been passing through Charnley Acre – for what reason exactly he hadn't said – but he'd come to see her, that was the important thing, the *lovely* thing. The whys and wherefores didn't matter.

And then, minutes after he'd arrived, he'd morphed into a stroppy teenager and looked down his nose at poor little Ramona like she was something the cat had brought in.

It wasn't as if she hadn't told him about Ramona beforehand, was it? And no, she wasn't going to ask the girl to leave before she'd finished her homework, which had been his first, outrageous, request. And *no*, that didn't mean she'd gone off him. He should have known that from the way she responded to his kiss. *Talk about insecure.* She'd wanted him, so much, at that moment; he must have been able to tell. But clearly, with her very welcome visitor in situ, it wasn't going to happen right away.

She could have accused him of being inconsiderate, or childish, or any of the other unsavoury attributes he'd displayed when he'd accused her of going cold on him. Instead, she'd tried to make light of it, and said something like, 'We can't always have what we want when we want it.' Or a playful variation of that, at any rate.

If he'd been patient and waited until Ramona had left of her own accord, they could have gone out to eat, then come back to the cottage and enjoyed a night of passion, or a long evening at any rate. But her suggestion had fallen on stony ground. He didn't have time to go out to dinner, he told her. He had 'things to do' later, apparently. And anyway, he'd had a long day and was too tired to drive around looking for somewhere to eat.

But not too tired for sex, apparently.

In the end, he'd calmed down about it, as Emily had, too. She'd had to; she didn't want a big falling-out. He'd kissed her again, rather perfunctorily, before coming up with a compromise which would involve him sloping off and doing whatever 'things' were so urgent, then he'd come back to hers around ten.

No dinner date, no companionable evening, only bed. Well, it wasn't a compromise that worked for Emily. When she said she'd rather leave it until tomorrow, Saturday – *if* he was free – and spend some proper time together, he hadn't sounded pleased but he'd seemed to be making an effort to be accepting. Not that he should have to make an effort with her.

She'd had a text from him first thing this morning apologising for being such a bad-tempered grouch, and he'd see her later, if she was still free. If so, he'd come to hers around 6 pm, then take her out to dinner, if that was okay with her. At least he had asked, not just assumed, which was a step in the right direction.

She'd said yes straight away. It was just too tiring to play it any differently.

'We're having a barbecue, just the family. A last minute thing, it's such a gorgeous day,' Laura said when she rang Emily on Sunday morning. 'You'll come, won't you? Bring Ethan if you like.' She gave a stilted little laugh. 'Well, of course you must bring Ethan.'

It wasn't the first time Emily had heard that tone in her friend's voice when she mentioned Ethan. It wasn't as if she didn't like him, Emily knew that, and he'd got on well with Clayton on the few occasions the four of them had got together. It was more to do with Laura's reservations about him being the right man for Emily.

And with good reason, she supposed.

Laura's astuteness and her natural concern for her friend probably meant she'd picked up on more than Emily had actually told her. So often, the truth showed itself not in what was said but what wasn't.

'Ethan's not here. I'm not seeing him today, he's busy. We went our separate ways last night, after we'd been out to dinner.' She kept her tone deliberately light and upbeat, as if it didn't matter to her one way or the other whether Ethan spent Sunday with her or not.

She didn't add that they'd had a bit of a contretemps last night – another one. It was her fault; she'd started it. It had been all right by the time they'd got their respective taxis home, though. On the surface, anyway.

But this morning she felt downhearted at the memory of last night. Her suggestion that they eat at one of the restaurants at the marina had been dismissed outright. She would have been happy to drive to Brighton, leave the car there and take a cab home, if necessary, or she could have stayed over in Ethan's apartment. On the odd occasion she'd stayed there, it had been lovely to wake up and look out at the sky and the sea, and the boats clustered in their moorings. It made a refreshing change from the countryside.

But no, that wasn't an option, apparently. Ethan hadn't even been willing to consider or even discuss her idea, as if she shouldn't have a say in where they went or what they did. He'd brushed it aside as if he was removing a piece of fluff from his jacket. Instead, he'd told her he'd booked a table at a bistro in Rottingdean, the seaside village halfway between Brighton and Cliffhaven. They'd been there before – the little place had great atmosphere and excellent food. But that wasn't the point.

She'd made it clear she was disappointed, and not a little annoyed that he hadn't thought to ask her where she'd like to go. He'd countered it by saying he thought she liked having a nice evening planned for her. He didn't add that most women would; he hadn't needed to. It was right there, in his voice, and his expression. That Ethan thought her ungrateful, which wasn't true at all, had needled her all the way to Rottingdean. They hardly spoke at all during the taxi ride. Again, her fault. Probably.

But she hadn't wanted to spoil their date, and she'd brightened up as they'd taken their table. Ethan had responded, reaching across the table, smiling into her eyes in a way guaranteed to make her feel she was the only other person in the room.

It was peace of a sort. It hadn't lasted.

The truth refused to be ignored any longer. As time went on, she and Ethan were seeing less of each other, not more, and it was time she faced up to that. She loved him, he loved her – or so he claimed – so why weren't they taking their relationship to the next level, becoming closer, even moving in together, or at least thinking about it? It wasn't as if they were in the first flush of youth. Emily felt young, both at heart and physically, but the plain fact was she was closer to fifty than forty, Ethan the same. So, what was the point of waiting? What were they waiting for, exactly?

And then there was the promised holiday to Italy – or anywhere – she didn't mind where they went as long as they were together. It hadn't warranted a mention last night, or any other night recently, and for some reason, she hadn't felt she couldn't broach the subject directly.

But still, she couldn't just sit there and say nothing, however badly it ended.

She'd put down her glass of Merlot with a deliberate movement and looked across the flickering faux-flame of the candle.

'Ethan, is everything okay? With us, I mean?'

He'd looked up from his panna cotta in surprise. 'Of course. Why wouldn't it be?' He'd sounded defensive, guilty even. Unless she'd imagined that.

She'd explained how she'd been feeling, choosing her words carefully, rubbing her finger gently on his hand as it rested on the table.

'We don't seem to be making any headway, Ethan, and I'm not sure what to make of that,' she'd ended.

And then, in a manner which had become typical of him, Ethan's handsome face had broken into an appealing smile, his eyes – his whole attention – focussed solely on her as he apologised again for not spending enough time with her. When the business truly got off the ground and he could be sure it could stand the expense, he'd farm the designs out to more freelancers. 'Then the world will be ours.'

'But do you see a future for us, a long-term future?'

She'd been pushing it, she could tell that by his expression. But she deserved to have some idea of how he saw their relationship progressing, and didn't regret the question.

'Nobody knows what the future holds, Emily.' He'd drained his wine glass, very fast.

'I know, but...'

'I want to be with you, Em. No doubt about it. You want to be with me, don't you?'

'Of course I do. I love you.'

'And I love you. So, let's just be patient, eh?' he'd said, effectively closing down the conversation.

'I'm tired,' she'd told him as they left the bistro and strolled down the narrow street towards the sea and the taxi rank. 'I'll be off home, if you don't mind.' *Alone*, she meant.

'You're angry with me,' had been his immediate, rather sharp, response. 'I said I was sorry. I will make it up to you. And we will have that holiday we talked about. Just not right now.'

'No, I'm not angry. It's fine, I get it,' she'd lied. This was all getting far too wearing, and her tiredness was genuine. 'We've got our own lives and our careers. We don't need to be in each other's pockets all the time, do we?'

Had she been testing him by saying that? She didn't know. If it was a test, Ethan had passed it, if not with an A star then a fairly respectable B.

'I wish I could live in your pocket, then I'd be close to you all the time,' he'd said, chuckling.

Then he'd tugged her into a shop doorway, tilted her chin with his forefinger, and kissed her, thoroughly, tenderly, sexily. She'd kissed him back with genuine, equal passion, for a moment regretting that she hadn't asked him back to Cloud Cottage.

But they were only words. Easy.

'You really love him, don't you?' Laura looked sideways at Emily. She broke off a hunk of baguette and handed it to Daisy, her almost-two-year-old granddaughter. The toddler hurtled down the grassy slope, blonde ponytail bouncing, straight into the arms of Holly, her mother, before stuffing the bread into her mouth.

'Yes, I do love him. Unfortunately.' She laughed. 'I don't mean unfortunately. Not really. You can't help who you fall for.'

She'd given Laura a potted version of last night's date with Ethan and their unsatisfactory discussion about their future – if they had one.

'Keep your eyes and ears open,' was all that Laura said, although what Emily should be watching and listening for she didn't say. 'Don't let him take advantage.'

'I won't.' Emily nodded. 'I promise.' It was a promise she'd made to herself, as well as her friend.

She picked up a sprig of watercress from her plate and put it down again. 'Something strange happened, though. At least, I thought it was strange. When Ethan turned up on Friday afternoon, okay, he was only after one thing, he made that pretty clear. And why not? It's flattering to be desired, and it's not as if I didn't want it, too. We're both adults.'

'Go on. I'm listening,' Laura said, widening her eyes comically and glancing around to check the others weren't within hearing distance.

Emily giggled. 'You're not getting any juicy details. Sorry.'

'Dammit. What, then?'

Emily sighed. 'It's the way he acted with Ramona. It was true that her being there put paid to anything we might have got up to, of course, but it's not as if we don't have plenty of other opportunities and I've got used to having her around. No, it was the way he looked at her. He didn't crack a smile when I took him in to meet her and it was all he could do to grunt at her. I didn't expect him to chat – she was in the middle of her homework – but a few friendly words wouldn't have gone amiss. Instead, he had a face like thunder. I could see she was puzzled. She was probably wondering what she'd done wrong, poor girl.'

Laura was thoughtful. 'That was a bit strange, like you say. Okay, he hadn't expected Ramona to be there spoiling his plans, so that must have been why he was off with her, but he didn't need to behave like that. He was plain rude, by the sound of it.'

'Yes, well, he needs to bloody well grow up,' Emily said, with a firm little nod. 'Mind you, he's not the first bloke I've said that about.'

Laura's mouth twisted before she let out a laugh. 'Sorry. Not funny.'

But Emily was laughing too. She felt better now. Talking to Laura, having a giggle, was working its magic. Already, her worries about Ethan were diminishing.

Laura got up and walked towards the house. A few minutes later, she was back with two glasses of Prosecco. She handed one to Emily. 'I wasn't going to drink this afternoon, with the little one around and everything, but I think we deserve this.'

CHAPTER 13

Spindlewood's extensive gardens were mainly on a slope, rising gently to a wild, wooded area at the back, and downwards to the gates at the front. Over the years, the undulations had caused many a gardener problems when mowing the lawn, but Clayton had it down to a fine art. A gardener by trade, he owned a hugely successful business called Green and Fragrant Gardening Services. They were in the back garden now, on a flattish piece of lawn beyond the rose garden with its arches smothered in fragrant blooms. Beyond the boundary hedge, tall trees, alive with birdsong, stood sentinel against the backdrop of a blue-and-white sky.

Emily sat back, sipped her wine and gazed around, taking pleasure in the sights and sounds of an English country garden. There were worst places to be.

'It all wants watering again,' Laura said, with a sigh. 'All this dry weather. It's hard to keep up. Still, I expect Clayton will put the sprinklers on tonight.'

Hearing his name mentioned, her husband came over, holding aloft the fork from the barbecue like a manic chef. 'Can I tempt anyone to the last of the chicken? Emily?'

'Ah, no thanks... oh, go on then. I'd hate to see it going to waste.'

Clayton returned to the gas barbecue and threw more chicken onto the grill.

'He's happy doing that,' Emily observed.

'Yep. Loves it,' Laura said. 'It suits me not to have to cook on a Sunday. Any excuse. Same for you, Holl, isn't it?'

'God, yes. We do share the cooking, though, Isaac and me.'

Holly, Laura's daughter, was nearby, Daisy in her arms. They were so alike, those two. They had the same delicate features, pale blonde hair and grey-blue eyes, just like Laura. The baby had been dark haired when she was born but had gradually grown fairer, and now mother, daughter, and granddaughter were like three peas from the same pod. Isaac wasn't Daisy's biological father, but he was the only one she'd known, and he loved her with an almost ferocious protectiveness.

He was at the barbecue now, chatting to Clayton. They made such a lovely family, Emily thought. Laura Engleby and Clayton Masters had found one another five years after Laura's husband, James, died. They were so well suited, those two. Once they'd set eyes on each other, their future together seemed inevitable, although others had worked that out before the couple themselves had. Holly and Isaac had got together at a pivotal time in Holly's life when she'd just become a single mother. It showed how life could turn around on a sixpence and happiness grew and blossomed when it was least expected.

Perhaps it would be the same for her, Emily mused. Meeting Ethan had seemed like fate after a somewhat frantic spell of internet dating which, in the end, had come to nothing. She remembered saying so to him at the time and Ethan, with two serious relationships under his belt, had felt the same.

It hadn't been easy to start all over again, for either of them. Ethan hadn't been specific about why he and his last girlfriend had parted. She'd prompted him a little, out of natural curiosity, but he seemed not to want to talk about it and she'd understood him not wanting to resurrect the past.

Clayton came over and levered a crisp, golden piece of chicken from the fork onto Emily's plate. She thanked him, and when he'd gone back to his cooking, she looked across at Laura.

'So, what I'm thinking is,' Emily began, taking up the threads of their earlier conversation, 'perhaps Ethan doesn't want to rush things simply because he wants it to work out. We've both got history, we're both at the stage where we're looking for a life partner. We have to be sure we've got it right this time.'

Laura, who'd been lying back in her chair, sat up and looked at Emily. '*Really*, Em? You believe that's what the go-slow is about?'

'I honestly don't know. He hasn't said that, but that doesn't mean he isn't thinking it.'

'Second-guessing what's in each other's minds doesn't make for closeness, does it?' Laura said, her expression doubtful. 'If that's the case, why doesn't he just come out and say so?'

'Because he doesn't want to hurt me, make me doubt that he loves me?'

Her theory made sense, more so now she'd voiced it. Besides, she couldn't carry on picking away at her relationship, looking for snags that may not be there. It didn't make her happy, doing that.

Laura lay back again and put her bare feet up on the footrest. 'It's possible, I guess. You know him better than I do. He's the first man since Mitch you've fallen in love with properly, so of course you want to hang on in there. Well, you go for it, girl, but like I said, don't let him take advantage.' She reached down beside her chair for the Prosecco. 'Top up?'

Ethan phoned at seven o'clock on Sunday evening. Emily could have sworn she heard birds chirruping in the background, and they definitely weren't seagulls.

'Are you at home, at the marina?' she asked, after he'd enquired about her day and she'd told him about her afternoon with Laura and her family at Spindlewood.

'Yes, of course I am,' Ethan said. 'I've been roughing out ideas for a new company's logo. I've been at it so long I didn't realise the time. Why do you ask?'

'No reason.'

Perhaps it wasn't birdsong she'd heard. It could have been the television. Remembering her new resolve to be watchful but stay positive, she smiled into the handset, as if he could see.

'We'll have a cosy night in at mine this week. I'll cook – that's a promise, not a threat.' She laughed. 'Only if you're free, of course. Otherwise I'll see you when I see you.'

Oh dear, that sounded awful, as if she couldn't care less. Ethan didn't seem to notice. He was talking quite fast, telling her how spectacular the sunset over the marina was, but his voice was getting lower and lower and she couldn't catch every word.

'I love you,' Emily said, when he'd stopped talking.

'Love you more.' He was gone.

On Monday, Ramona came to Cloud Cottage after school. She'd arrived a little before Emily. Emily had shown her where the spare key to the front door was kept – round the back, under a large stone in the flower bed, halfway up the garden. She trusted Ramona, and there didn't seem any point in stopping her from coming just because Emily was going to be home later. She never got back much after five, anyway, unless she was out on a reporting assignment, in which case she texted Ramona and told her not to come. The loose arrangement worked on both sides, and she had to admire the way the girl got down to her homework and ploughed on until she'd finished, only stopping to devour a steady supply of drinks and snacks provided by Emily. She seemed so hungry all the time. Emily could remember herself at that age, always starving, buying cakes and chocolate on the way home from school and still managing to tuck away a big, home-cooked dinner later.

It could have been her imagination, but Ramona seemed to have lost a little weight since she'd started coming here; not that there'd been much of her in the first place. And yet, thankfully, there was no sign of her being on any sort of diet, judging the way she polished off the sandwiches, biscuits, and fruit Emily left out for her. Her hair looked as if it could do with a wash, too, Emily noticed. It wasn't dirty, as such, but not as shiny-clean as it used to be. It hung limply like rat's tails over the collar of her school shirt.

'Is everything okay with you?' Emily asked, when Ramona closed her geography file with a satisfied sigh. 'Did you have a good weekend?'

The girl considered this carefully, as she considered everything, before she gave her customary serious answer.

'Yes, I did. On Saturday I went to Cliffhaven, shopping, and in the evening I watched *Bridesmaids* on DVD, which is a 15 but Mum lets me watch it, and on Sunday I went for a walk.'

'That's nice. Did you go shopping with your mum?'

'Yes... oh no, I forgot, I went with Lilah, my friend from my class. She got a new lipstick and we both tried it out in the toilets in Marks. It looked cool on her but silly on me.'

'Oh, I'm sure that's not true. I bet you looked great.'

Ramona tilted her head to one side. 'I might have. I couldn't tell.'

Emily smiled. 'You're a funny one. Funny in a good way, I mean.'

'Yes, I know.' Ramona smiled, too – a proper, amused smile. She didn't smile very often, Emily realised.

'And how about your mum? Is she still getting her books from the library in the village?'

'I *think* so.' The serious look was back. 'What dog is that, in the photo?'

Ramona was looking at the black-and-white framed photo on the wall next to the window.

'That's Wilf. He was my whippet. He died last year. He was quite old.'

'He looks nice. I expect he was good company,' Ramona said, a wistful look in her eyes.

'He was my faithful companion for years,' Emily said. 'I'd had him since he was a puppy.'

'You could get another dog. You should, if you miss him.'

'Maybe I will.' Emily said.

CHAPTER 14

Karen fastened the buttons on her blue nurse's tunic and changed wedge-heeled sandals for flat black shoes, ready to begin the day shift at Seaview House. She peered into the mirror on the wall, frowning at what she saw: a face etched with tiredness. It wasn't easy, single-parenting a wilful sixteen-year-old girl and keeping on top of the housework when all she wanted to do when she got home from work was stuff her face with comfort food, sink a large glass of wine and fall into bed.

But she didn't complain, at least, hardly ever. The poor souls in her care had much more to complain about.

She was tweaking her fringe into place when she noticed two creases deepening either side of her mouth. They weren't there before, surely? She wasn't even forty yet, for God's sake! Perhaps it was a trick of the light. The sun squeezed sideways through the small, too high window of the staff area, yellowy and inadequate. A trick of the light, that's what it was. Karen smiled at her reflection. The creases turned into laughter lines. Better. Taking a tube of concealer from her handbag, she dabbed a fingerful onto a spot that had erupted on her chin overnight. Better again.

Whatever, she'd have to do.

Saleema arrived, having just come off duty.

'I saw the doctor's car leaving as I came in,' Karen said, kicking her sandals under a chair. 'Has there been a drama?'

Saleema looked up from her mobile phone. 'Drama? Not really. He came for Mrs Donnelly. She's had another one of her TIAs by the looks of it. It's hard to be sure once it's come and gone. She's got a slight chest infection, too. The doctor gave her the once-over, put her on antibiotics, and upped her other meds.'

'Not a hospital job, then?'

'Nope.' Saleema dropped her mobile into her bag and zipped it up. 'She'd only be stuck on a trolley in a corridor for hours and there's nothing they can do that hasn't been done already. She's better off here with us. I expect the doc'll pop in again.'

'Sad, isn't it?' Karen said. 'She's such a darling and she's got nobody as far as we know. She's not had a single visitor since she got here.'

'She's got spirit, I'll say that for her.' Saleema slammed the warped metal door of her locker shut and turned the key. 'The doc was talking to her earlier and she was answering him. Some of what she said actually made sense. I heard her say something about Caroline again. She's keeps on saying that name. Has anyone bothered to find out, I wonder?'

Karen shrugged. 'I doubt it.'

On her way along the green-painted corridor to begin her duties, Karen popped her head round the office door. Adam, the administrator, was at his desk, which was practically invisible due to the chaotic piles of paperwork, the corners of which were lifting in the breeze from the open window. He turned from the computer screen, swivelling round on the revolving chair. The sun glossed the pink skin where his hairline had begun to recede.

'Hiya. What can I do you for?'

'Mrs Donnelly, the woman in one of the NHS beds. Transfer from Cliffhaven General. Do you have anything new on her?'

'Should I have?'

Karen came right into the room. 'It's only that she's still not had any visitors, and nobody seems to know much about her.'

Adam rattled his asthma inhaler and drew noisily on it before swinging back to the screen. 'Hang on.' He tapped at the keyboard.

Karen waited.

'We seem to have an address for her,' Adam said, after a minute. 'The hospital got it from her GP, by the looks of it. An address, which might not be up to date, of course, and her date of birth, which puts her a month shy of eighty-two. Other than that, zilch. It's not my job to complete the picture.'

He followed this with a smile to temper the comment, probably in case Karen was thinking he hadn't done his job properly, which she wasn't. It was crisis management all the way; patients' medical welfare first. Anything else... well, there wasn't the time, let alone the money, for anything else.

'The only name she's mentioned is Caroline, but it doesn't mean there is such a person. You know how it is.'

Adam looked at the on-screen record again. 'I do. Anyway, there's nothing here about a Caroline. I'll stick a note on.'

'Ta. A social worker must have been assigned by now, though. Perhaps they'll do something.'

Adam gave Karen a long, pointed look.

She grinned. 'Yeah, okay. Don't hold your breath.' She nodded at the inhaler. 'In your case, definitely don't.'

'Ha, ha, very funny.' Adam stuck his tongue out at her.

Karen glanced at the clock on the wall above Adam's head and hurried away to her patients.

Across the other side of town, Glenda Robertson, social worker, pulled onto a petrol station forecourt, filled the car with fuel and picked up an Americano and an almond croissant when she went inside to pay. This was breakfast; she was running late today because the twins had refused to co-operate over the simple matter of getting dressed, then fought in the back seat all the way to school.

Glenda had made the usual threat, raising her voice above the racket – 'Wait till your dad gets home. It'll be straight to bed with no tea and no football on Saturday!' Allies once more, the boys had giggled and nudged each other. They knew a hollow threat when they heard one. Glenda had handed them over to the Year Two class teacher with a sigh of relief and a sympathetic smile.

She took a sip of coffee then propped the paper cup on the passenger seat, with the croissant in its paper bag. A little way on, she came to a handy grass verge. It wouldn't hurt to take ten minutes before her first call of the day, to a young, newly-delivered mum whose partner had just been sentenced to two years in prison for his part in an armed robbery.

The croissant tasted good, the coffee even better. It wasn't the healthiest of breakfasts, especially for somebody carrying a certain amount of extra weight, as she was, but, well, nobody was looking, were they?

The empty coffee cup and croissant wrapper stowed in the glove compartment, along with the telltale wrappers from previous energy-giving snacks, Glenda brushed pastry crumbs from the front of her navy blue cardigan, took out her phone and checked her messages. There was one sent ten minutes ago from Adam, the administrator at Seaview House, asking about a Mrs Matilda Donnelly. Glenda had to think who he meant for a moment. She had no mind picture; the case was a new one, and she hadn't had a chance to meet the lady concerned yet. She reached for her work bag on the back seat and sifted through the paperwork it contained. Yes, there was the file – a thin one, with only one sheet of paper inside it.

Adam was asking if any relatives of Mrs Donnelly had come to light, or anyone else who might have an interest in her. There was a question mark over somebody called Caroline, apparently. The message included the information that Mrs Donnelly was poorly but stable, which Glenda would have noted before and not given the case a high priority. But because of Adam's query, she read through what it said on the file. There was an address, a date of birth, and a brief description of the circumstances of the hospital admission and the subsequent transfer to Seaview. That was all. If there was a relative who may or may not be called Caroline Donnelly, it should be possible to track her down. Possible, but time-consuming. And not really anyone's job.

Glenda tapped out a reply to Adam: *Do we have a landline phone number for that address?*

It wasn't until late morning, after she'd made three home visits and had almost reached the grey, pebbledash building in Cliffhaven where the office was that Adam's reply came through. *Yup, you're in luck. She's listed.* He followed this with the number.

Glenda sat in the office car park, intending to call Mrs Donnelly's home in Charnley Acre now, as Adam presumably had not done, or he would have said. She was about to press in the number when another call came through. She took it. It was the mother of one of the patients she was booked in to see next week, with a query about her son's support worker. Something else she needed to sort out, or rather, add to her ever-growing list of things to sort out.

Glenda pushed the phone back into her bag. Mrs Donnelly and her mystery relative – if there was one – could wait a bit longer. Anyway, if she managed to see the lady herself meanwhile, the question might be answered, although there was no guarantee of that, of course.

Time was getting on. Glenda locked the car and went into the office, where she wasn't in the least surprised to find she'd been allocated two more cases, both of them sounding like high priority. And none had dropped off the other end. Of course they hadn't.

The thin file on Mrs Matilda Donnelly found itself back at the bottom of the pile.

CHAPTER 15

Three weeks. *Three whole weeks!* Would Tilly ever come home? Of course, she would. Three weeks was nothing. Time stretched or shrunk, according to your mood; she'd always found that.

Ramona gave herself a good talking-to inside her head. Tilly used to do that – correction, Tilly *does* that – tells herself not to be a daft old bat if ever her thoughts run off in a direction they've no place to be. 'I'm a daft old bat, I am!' Ramona could hear her saying it now. They'd have a right laugh about whatever it was Tilly's mind had been turning cartwheels over. Ramona laughed now, into the empty space of the kitchen. It wasn't the same as laughing with Tilly but it made her feel better. More in charge. Because she *was* in charge, wasn't she? She was in full charge of Number One The Pasture, and of herself. And she was making a pretty good job of it, even if she said so herself. Ramona nodded firmly over the sinkful of washing up that had waited a day longer than it should have done.

It was becoming a nuisance as well as dead hard work, heating up water in the kettle all the time, especially when she wanted to have a bath. All the to-ing and fro-ing could take half the evening, and even then, the water only just about covered her knees. She'd discovered that the big saucepan, the one Tilly used to make jam, held loads more than the kettle, but it took longer to heat up on the cooker ring, and it wasn't so easy to carry either. But there, that was the choice. The kettle or the pan. Take it or leave it. Tilly said that, too, about any number of things. *Take it or leave it.*

It was Friday evening. At least Ramona didn't have to think about what to have for dinner; she'd gone to Lilah's house after school and Lilah's dad had gone to the chippy for fish and chips for everyone. Afterward they'd eaten, they'd had a riotous time playing cricket in the long back garden with Lilah's little sister, Sophie, and two of her brothers, Olly and Tim – the ones who were nearest in age to Lilah. They were a good laugh, those two, when they weren't being a pain, which Lilah maintained was most of the time.

It was getting dark by the time Ramona had caught the bus home. Lilah's mum had worried about that, and offered Lilah's dad to run her home in the car. But she'd said, no, she'd be fine, thank you very much. And yes, she had let her gran know what time to expect her, so she could keep a look-out for the bus.

'I never saw you ring your gran,' Lilah had said, right in front of everyone, her face all sort of accusing.

'I did it outside, when you'd come in to use the loo.'

The answer had tripped off her tongue, as easily as that. The offer of the lift had been tempting, but too risky. Lilah's dad might have wanted to see her right to the door, and wondered why there were no lights on and no sign of her gran. Ramona was sure her brain had sharpened up since all this happened. It certainly went fast enough when she needed it to, which was a good thing, wasn't it? Having her brain speeded up could help a lot in her end-of-term exams.

Which reminded her. Emily said she could go to Cloud Cottage tomorrow if she wanted to, even though it was Saturday. She'd told Emily about the exams, and how she needed to revise really hard. Emily had asked about her brothers, and whether they were revising for exams, too, and if they had the same problem as her, with too many people in the house. That had been a sticky moment because Ramona couldn't remember exactly how much detail she'd given Emily about her – Lilah's – brothers. She must have said some of them were still at school, otherwise Emily wouldn't be asking that question. She'd fudged her answer, muttering something about them going into trades and not needing that many exams, which was actually close to the truth, if it *had* been Lilah's brothers they were talking about.

Emily had raised her eyebrows but hadn't asked any more questions. They were there, all the same, hiding behind her smiley face. Ramona resolved to be even more careful about what she said.

It was all getting rather complicated, but Ramona loved spending time at Cloud Cottage. And having Emily as a friend made her feel safe, even if the whole thing was based on fibs. She would go there tomorrow, just for the morning – Emily had said to come in the morning, because she was going out with Ethan in the afternoon. Ethan was definitely Emily's boyfriend. Ramona hadn't been sure at first but now she was, from the way Emily said his name. You could tell a lot from the way somebody said a person's name.

'Ramona, are you sure your parents don't mind you coming here? They've never met me, after all. As far as they're concerned, I'm a complete stranger.'

This came before Ramona had set her work out on the table. She was in the kitchen while Emily made her a hot chocolate.

She had the distinct impression that Emily had planned that question before she got here.

'No, they don't mind at all. They're very grateful I've got somewhere quiet to study. I said before. They said to say thank you.'

Ramona picked up her drink and went to take it through to the living room. But Emily wasn't finished with the questions yet.

'Your mum never did ring me, though. Could you leave me her number before you go? I think it's a good idea if I have a little chat with her, don't you? Maybe later?'

'She's busy today. She's taken my little sister, Sophie, to the dentist and then they're going shopping, or something.'

'The dentist? On a Saturday?'

'Yes, it saves her missing school. And this afternoon she's taking my brothers to some car racing thing.'

Lilah's elder brothers were crazy about cars and engines. Ramona knew they went to watch banger racing, whatever that was.

'Didn't your father want to go to that?' Emily asked.

'He can't. He's working all day. He's a policeman.' As was Lilah's dad.

Suddenly, she was so tempted – *so* tempted – to blurt out the truth, confess to Emily that it was all lies, and really she'd been left on her own with nobody to turn to, nobody to look out for her. And then, just as suddenly, she remembered what this was all about. It was about her being grown up and taking responsibility while her grandmother was in Seaview House, recovering from being a little bit unwell and having a good old rest while she was doing it. There was nothing wrong with that, was there? All Ramona had to do was hang on in there and wait for everything to go back to normal. She was fine as she was, and there was nothing for anyone to get in a sweat about.

She smiled brightly at Emily.

'Right, I see,' Emily said, dragging out the word. 'Well, I'd better let you get on. Ethan's due around twelve so...'

So, she was to be out of the way by then. Fine. She had no intention of playing gooseberry, neither did she particularly want Emily's boyfriend to get all annoyed when he'd only just arrived. That could spoil Emily's day, which would be awful if it was all Ramona's fault.

She didn't like Ethan. Okay, she didn't know him but her gut told her she didn't like him, and that was that. She wished Emily had a different boyfriend. Somebody with better manners, for a start.

An hour later, Ramona had filled in her science revision sheets, finished her geometry and read a few more pages of *Lord of the Flies*. It was while she was flicking through her history text book that she realised she was spinning out her visit. Her homework was up to date, and she'd done so much revision because of her sessions at Cloud Cottage that she felt her brain would burst clean out of her skull if she crammed any more into it. Anyway, supposing Ethan turned up early? It was only a quarter past eleven, but if he was really *into* Emily – one of Lilah's expressions – he might not want to wait another moment to see her.

She stood up and put her pens and pencils back in the case, with the lucky mouse or shrew skull. As she began to fill her rucksack with her files and books, she realised something else: she didn't want to stay here any longer today. Those questions Emily had asked her, well, it wasn't the first time, was it? And she'd gone all sort of thoughtful, like there was a lot more she wanted to know but was saving it for another day. It felt kind of awkward now, as if at any moment, Emily might come out with something that would catch Ramona right off-guard.

A vision of the social people putting her into a car – or

would it be a van? – and carting her off to some terrible institution ran across her line of sight, like a horror film. It could happen, if the truth came out, it really could. The vision was yet another reminder that she must stay strong, and focussed. It wouldn't be for much longer.

'I'll be off now,' she called up the stairs. 'Bye!'

'Hang on!' Emily appeared at the top of the stairs. She was wearing a sort of robe thing and her hair was wrapped up in a towel. Ramona wondered if she was going to remind her about leaving the phone number. Instead, she just laughed, and pointed at the towel, which had a chestnut-coloured stain on the front. 'Look at the state of me, I'm in the middle of doing my colour.'

Ramona wondered about Emily's timing. Wasn't she cutting it fine, with her boyfriend due?

'He might come early,' she said. 'Ethan might. And find you with your hair all wet.'

'Yep, he might.' Emily grinned. 'But I doubt it. If he does, he can take me as he finds me.'

Ramona smiled, and nodded her approval. For a moment, it seemed as if she and Emily were conspirators in taking sides against Ethan, like sharing a secret. It gave her a warm feeling inside.

She said goodbye to Emily again, and left by the front door. She'd only just closed the garden gate and walked a short way along Hammerpot Lane when a car appeared and she moved closer to the edge of the lane for safety. The car slowed as it approached Cloud Cottage and she recognised Ethan at the wheel. Her premonition that he'd arrive early had come true. She wondered if he'd find Emily with her head over the wash basin? Well, it served him right if he did. He'd just have to wait until she was ready for him.

As he passed by, he turned his head and looked right at her.

The lane was narrow and for that second they'd been really close up. He must have recognised her, and yet he'd totally ignored her. No smile, no toot of the horn, or anything. He may not like her, but she was Emily's friend. Politeness costs nothing, as Tilly said.

'Well, stuff you,' Ramona said out loud. If Lilah was here, they'd have said *stuff you* about a million times and turned it into a chant. Once would do for now. It wasn't an expression Tilly would approve of – unless she used it herself, in which case it was perfectly okay.

Ramona took the longer route home, walking right along the high street instead of taking the turning before it. She felt like being in the open air. First thing this morning, the clouds had piled up in the sky, looking like extra grey hills above the Downs. There'd even been a few spots of rain. But now the sky was back to summer blue, and the remaining clouds had turned white and puffy and harmless.

Her rucksack bounced against her shoulders as she walked along, looking in the shop windows. Being amongst the Saturday morning shoppers and the summer visitors, Ramona felt anonymous. Nobody knew her in the village because she spent so much time away from it – at home, or at school, or at Lilah's. That could be a bad thing, or it could be good, depending on how you looked at it. Whichever it was, right now it served Ramona's purpose to a T.

By the time she'd arrived home, two things had happened. Firstly, the postman had been. There were already some letters – official, boring-looking things – addressed to Tilly, which Ramona was storing in the brass letter rack, waiting for Tilly to come home and open them. But this time it was a postcard. It was addressed to Tilly, and really, Ramona shouldn't be reading it. With a postcard, though, you couldn't help seeing what was on it, could you?

She looked first at the picture of Niagara Falls and then, turning the card over, she read:

Dear Tilly, sorry did not get to see you before we went. All such a rush and tear! Having a wonderful time here. Seeing my sister after all these years is marvellous. Six whole weeks in Canada, I can hardly believe it! We brought one of the kids with us in the end, otherwise we'd never have made the trip if we'd waited for the next gap. You know how it is, one goes and another one comes, bless them. Hope you're fine. See you when we get back. Give my love to Ramona. Mary (and Richard) xx

That was kind of Tilly's friend, sending Ramona her love. The postcard was a huge relief, too. Ramona had been trying not to think about Mary. You couldn't worry about everything, but in the back of her mind she'd thought Mary must be wondering why her friend hadn't been to visit lately, or phoned. But it was fine, because now she knew that Mary had gone on holiday, all the way to Canada for six weeks, so was none the wiser. Ramona gave silent thanks for this piece of luck.

She went to put the card in the letter rack, then changed her mind and propped it up against a plant pot on the kitchen windowsill as a welcome for Tilly. The bit Mary had written about kids coming and going didn't make sense to her, but no doubt it would mean something to her grandmother.

The second thing was that there was a message on the landline answerphone. Somehow, in her tidying efforts, she'd pushed the phone to the back of the dresser where it sat behind a stack of crockery that had never made its way back into the cupboard, but now the red winking light caught her eye.

Ramona's first thought was '*Tilly*'. How long had the message been there? Her heart thumped as she cursed her stupidity for forgetting to check the phone for messages. Okay, her mobile phone was never far from her hand, but supposing Tilly or the hospital had tried to get in touch on the landline, and she hadn't noticed? Tilly had her mobile number but the hospital wouldn't have it, would they? She should have thought about that sooner. It seemed ridiculous now that she hadn't. Ridiculous – and *pathetic* – that she'd been waiting and waiting for somebody to get in touch about Tilly, and then she'd gone and let this happen!

She thought hard. When had she last checked the answerphone? There'd been a message about some delivery or other – a fake call, she could tell. The optician's had left a message about Tilly's appointment and Ramona had rung them and made some excuse to cancel. But that was last week!

Realising she was putting off listening to the new message because, suddenly, she was afraid of what she might hear, Ramona took a deep breath, pulled the machine forward and pressed the play button.

The message had come in only yesterday. It was from somebody called Glenda Robertson, who said she was... *a social worker*? Would somebody please call her back. Ramona sat down with a bump on the nearest chair. All the breath seemed to rush out of her lungs. Her heart raced. She felt sick. All the trouble she'd gone to, all that effort to cover her tracks and pretend that, as far as the doctors and nurses looking after Tilly were concerned, she didn't exist. And now this!

But how? She'd told nobody she was living here on her own. The only person who knew was Tilly herself, and she would never leave Ramona at the mercy of the authorities. Never *ever*.

Ramona took several deep breaths, played the message again, and applied logic to the situation. Was this Glenda person ringing to say they were bringing Tilly home? Did social workers do that sort of thing? She didn't think so. In fact, she was pretty sure that wasn't how it worked. Social workers were only involved if there was some sort of a problem.

Weren't they?

Ramona gazed into the wide, deep ravine of everything she didn't know. It was fathomless, black, and tremendously scary.

She sat for a while staring at the tiny white dot where the winking red light had been, and then, when her heart had gone back to more or less its normal speed, she fetched her mobile phone from her bag in the hall and rang Seaview House.

Putting on her best adult voice, she became Emily, though without giving the name.

'I was the person who rang the ambulance, when Til... Mrs Donnelly was first taken ill. I, well, everyone really... we were wondering if she was better now and if she's coming home soon?' Then she added, out of sheer panic, 'It is all right to ask that, isn't it?'

The female voice on the other end sounded brisk but distracted, as if she'd been in the middle of something important when she'd had to answer the phone.

'Well, you've asked it now. Hold on a minute, will you?'

Ramona held on for what seemed like a week. She was about to end the call, thinking she'd been cut off at the other end, when the voice returned.

'There isn't a lot I can tell you unless you're a relative, which you didn't say, so I'm assuming...'

'I'm not a relative,' Ramona said emphatically.

'Right, well, all I can tell you is that Mrs Donnelly is still poorly but she's comfortable.'

A bell screeched in the background. It sounded urgent.

'So, Mrs Donnelly isn't being sent home yet?'

'Oh no, dear. I'd say that's unlikely. *Highly* unlikely. Goodbye.'

Ramona sat with her mobile in her hand, not knowing what to think. Tilly was poorly – well, obviously, otherwise they wouldn't be keeping her there. But poorly could mean anything. It could just mean she'd got a cold on her chest, like she had last winter. She was comfortable, which meant she wasn't in pain, or seriously ill or anything. She imagined Tilly sitting up in bed with lots of pillows behind her, getting the rest she needed, and happily looking out at the view of the sea. It made Ramona feel better, imagining that. More in control. Actually, she felt *completely* in control now. Right back where she ought to be.

She got up from the chair and unplugged the landline from its socket.

CHAPTER 16

'Ethan, I refuse to be ravished with my hair all wet. Behave, will you?' Emily pushed him playfully away, laughing.

Ethan was laughing, too, grabbing Emily from behind as she scuttled away from him towards the stairs. He managed to claim a kiss before she escaped completely.

'I love you, wet hair or no wet hair. What's a man to do when you're so irresistible?' He gave a theatrical shrug.

'Be patient, that's what. Make yourself useful and put the coffee on while I go and dry off.'

She could hear him humming a tune as she ran upstairs to her bedroom, plugged in the hairdryer and reached for her blow-dry brush. She had the feeling this was going to be a good day. They hadn't seen each other during the week so she hadn't got to cook him the meal she'd promised, but he'd been busy, she got that, and so had she, and she'd tried not to read anything into his absence.

But today he'd arrived earlier than arranged, having finished whatever it was he had to do sooner than he'd expected, and in a pleasingly buoyant mood. They were going out for the day, then coming back to Cloud Cottage this evening for dinner. She'd prepared the food while Ramona was doing her homework, stuffing chicken breasts with cream cheese and herbs, peeling vegetables, and hulling strawberries which she would add to a meringue shell with cream to make a pavlova. It would save time later. And – miracle of miracles – Ethan was staying over.

She was supposed to have been attending a charity concert tonight and writing it up for the *Cliffhaven News,* but she'd persuaded a colleague to cover it instead. She'd done the same for him recently, and the editor was fine about swapping as long as the deadlines were met.

The things we do for love, Emily sang softly into the antique gilt-framed mirror which stood on top of the chest of drawers.

While she was blow-drying her hair, her mind drifted back to Ramona. Her hair had looked better today, and it had been properly brushed, but Emily was even more sure now that the girl had lost weight. It was quite obvious, now she'd looked closely. The waistband of Ramona's short skirt was so loose it had twisted round so that the zip was in the wrong place, and the hem had come unstitched at the back and been fixed with a couple of staples. She'd still not left that phone number, either, Emily realised now. Her mind had been on Ethan at the time and she hadn't thought to mention it to Ramona again before she left.

Emily sighed. There was no point in raising her concerns to Ethan. He'd made it perfectly clear by his attitude, and in the briefest of conversations they'd had, that he thought she was an idiot for getting involved with the girl in the first place. Perhaps he had a point. With no contact from Ramona's parents, other than the brief note from her mother, and no way of getting in touch with them, Emily had only had a scant idea of her family situation. Perhaps there was more to it than met the proverbial eye. If it was true that her father was a police officer, would he not want to check out exactly who his daughter was associating with? That in itself seemed strange. The house was overcrowded and not exactly peaceful, she knew that much, but was there something else, another reason Ramona had latched onto Emily? Because, looking back, that was exactly what had happened.

Emily's invitation to Cloud Cottage had been made on impulse, it was true, but Ramona had seemed overjoyed at the offer – a little too overjoyed, maybe? After all, Emily had at that point been a complete stranger. She didn't like to believe she'd somehow been manipulated by the girl – she didn't seem capable of it – but she was also someone who knew what she wanted, and possessed the fire and determination to get it.

Emily finished her hair and unplugged the drier. She was probably overthinking the Ramona situation, as she did most things. Perhaps she would talk to Laura about it the next time they met. Meanwhile, she had her day with Ethan to look forward to.

The rain woke Emily on Sunday morning, peppering the windows with wind-driven fury. The sky was relentlessly slate-grey. A solitary bird wheeled past the window, struggling against the thermals. The change in the weather was disappointing after yesterday, which had been golden, and perfect.

She and Ethan had driven to Rye in Ethan's car, strolled up and down the steep cobbled streets and had lunch in a pretty pub garden. In one of the antique shops they'd passed, Emily had admired a metal figurine of a whippet which looked just like Wilf, and Ethan had promptly insisted on buying it for her. It cost more than it should have, to Emily's mind, and weighed an absolute ton, but he'd gamely lugged it about until they'd got back to the car. It was downstairs now, taking pride of place on the hearth.

Ethan stirred in his sleep. His hair was all mussed up, the way Emily liked it. She leaned over and gently kissed his cheek. He woke up and smiled.

'Hello, you,' he said.

'Hello. It's raining.'

'So I see. Never mind, it was a great day yesterday, wasn't it?'

'It was. I had a lovely day.' Emily smiled into Ethan's eyes. 'And a wonderful night.'

Holding her gaze, Ethan raised himself up and pulled her close, caressing her bare shoulders, kissing her, gently opening her mouth with his. They made love again, slowly and lazily, until their passion built and urgency took over.

If you lived here with me, Emily thought afterwards, *it would be like this all the time.* But she didn't voice it. This time with Ethan had been perfect, and it wasn't over yet. She mustn't spoil it now.

'Shall we go out for lunch, or would you rather stay here?' she asked, when they eventually made it downstairs and were having coffee and croissants. 'I would have cooked you a proper Sunday breakfast but it's too late now.'

Ethan chuckled. 'And whose fault is that?'

Emily flashed her eyes. 'I'd say it's even-stevens.'

'Actually, do you mind if I head off soon?' Ethan said, after a pause. 'There are a few things I want to get done, ready for Monday.'

'No, that's fine. I want to write up my library article anyway.'

She was the tiniest bit disappointed, but that was all. They'd had quality time together, the longest time he'd spent with her for ages. One day – the day she was sure would come, however long it took – they'd be together properly. She could wait until Ethan was ready.

She got up from the table and took their empty mugs to the sink.

'Look, the rain's easing off. Why don't you get going now? No point in getting a soaking if you don't need to.'

Ethan glanced out of the window. He stood up. 'Yep, I'll trot off, if you're sure that's okay?'

'Of course it is. I said. I'll see you in the week, maybe?' She kissed him briefly on the lips.

'I'll do my best.'

Ethan put his thumb to the side of Emily's mouth and wiped away a pastry crumb. The tender gesture made her smile. She went through to the hall, took Ethan's jacket off the hook and handed it to him.

He took the jacket from her, shrugging into it, glancing away from her as he dealt with the zip. 'Oh, by the way, Em, I meant to tell you last night. I'm going away, the week after next. It's a conference in Sheffield, about technology in design.'

'Oh, okay,' Emily said, a little uncertainly. 'You didn't say, but never mind.'

'I wasn't sure if I'd got a place, which is why I didn't mention it before.'

'Oh. Well, it's good you've got in. How long is it for?'

'The conference? It's two and a half days, I think, but I thought as I'm going all that distance I may as well take advantage and catch up with some old friends at the same time. Do a spot of touring around Yorkshire and meet up with some mates I haven't seen for yonks.'

But he didn't have time to have a holiday with her.

'Sounds great.' She forced a smile as, once again, the doubts flooded in, unwanted, but unstoppable.

Did he want to be with her or not? And more than that, did he really love her? Or, was she being clingy and selfish for not relishing the idea of another enforced separation with no idea as to how long it would be.

No, it *wasn't* selfish. Not once had Ethan considered how she might feel; at least, it didn't sound as if he had.

She opened the front door for him, wanting him gone before she said something she might regret.

'I'll text,' he said. He blew her a kiss.

'You do that.'

CHAPTER 17

At mid-morning break on Monday, Lilah was nowhere to be found. One minute, she and Ramona had been together, elbowing their way through the throng to add their geography homework to the pile, and the next, Lilah had vanished into thin air.

Ramona didn't think too much about it. After a perfunctory look about, she heard her name being called. She traced the voice to a group of girls from her class who were sitting in a loose circle on the grass behind the music block. As soon as she sat down, the damp from yesterday's rain immediately seeped through her skirt, but it was better than standing about on the concrete part of the campus, and more friendly.

Right now, Ramona needed friendly.

'No! I don't believe it! Tell me that's not who I think it is.'

They all looked at Mila, who had turned round and was gazing across the grass towards the gym building, shading her eyes with her hand.

'What? Who?' several voices uttered at once.

Ramona followed Mila's line of sight, as did everyone else.

Amid the chorus of exclamations, some less polite than others, Ramona stayed quiet as she took in the scene before her. Lilah was coming from the direction of the gym building, with Jamie Tate. Clearly they'd come from the back of the back of the block and they were *slinking* round the corner. There was no other word for it. Even from this distance, Ramona could see that their faces were pink. As they ventured out from the shadows of the building, they veered away from each other, walking ridiculously far apart, as if they'd never seen one another before in their lives.

'Well, there's no need to ask what *they've* been up to.' Mila let out a peal of delighted laughter.

'She's been after him for bloody months,' Aysha said. 'Or he's been after her. One or the other.'

'Or *both*,' Mila said. 'Looks like they both got lucky, anyway.'

'Doesn't surprise me,' somebody said.

'Yeah, she is the type. Always thought that,' somebody else added.

'Stop it!' They all turned to look at Ramona. 'Don't talk about Lilah like that.'

Mila shrugged. 'Okay, we were only *saying*.'

'They've probably been having a private chat, that's all.' Ramona tugged her short skirt down to as close to her knees as it would go. She suddenly felt oddly exposed, as if she was linked in some way to Lilah, and whatever she'd been up to with Jamie. 'It is allowed to talk to boys, you know. It doesn't always have to be about... love and stuff.'

But the others weren't really listening. The novelty of seeing Lilah and Jamie coming out from behind the gym – it was no secret what went on behind there – had already worn off.

The bell sounded for next lesson. Ramona walked straight into school without looking around for Lilah, as if she needed to make a point – not that anyone would have noticed, least of all Lilah herself. Ramona couldn't help feeling sidelined, though. Best friend or not, it felt weird that Lilah had preferred to spend her break with some boy rather than her. Not in a jealous way, but weird, as in new and unknown – and different. If Lilah was by her side now, Ramona wouldn't know what to say to her. That in itself made her feel all scratchy and uncomfortable.

She didn't see Lilah for the rest of the day – they were in separate lessons. Ramona had choir practice at lunchtime and to save time, and money, she'd brought a packed lunch instead of using the canteen. After school, she waited in their usual place, by the pillar of the main gate. She waited for ages, until the crowd had thinned right out, but Lilah didn't appear. They always walked to Ramona's bus stop together. Lilah wouldn't have gone without her, which could only mean she was still inside school.

Unless she'd abandoned Ramona in favour of Jamie.

Nerves skittered through her stomach; she wasn't used to relying on anyone except herself, and Tilly, of course. But these days, the closeness and company seemed desperately important. Ramona swallowed hard to press the nervy feeling away, then turned through the gates and walked back to the school building.

She walked quickly along the corridor, avoiding the eye of any passing teachers, and checked the ground floor toilets. They seemed empty at first. A faulty tap dripped steadily into the echoey silence. Ramona waited uncertainly, then, after a minute, she heard a muffled sob. The end cubicle door was locked.

'Lilah? Is that you?'

A sniff, and then, 'I'm okay. Go away.'

'Of course I'm not going away! What's happened? Why are you crying?'

Silence, apart from another sniff.

Ramona stood close to the locked door, listening, waiting. Eventually, the lock clicked, the door creaked open and Lilah came out.

'He's not out there, is he?' She gazed fearfully towards the door to the corridor.

'I take it you mean Jamie. No, he's not there. No-one's there.'

'What about outside?'

'I didn't see him. He would have gone by now.' As had Ramona's bus, but this was far more important, and it wasn't as if there was anyone waiting for her at home. 'The cleaners will be here in a minute. Come on. Don't worry, I won't leave you.' Ramona put an arm round her friend's shoulders, still in the dark as to what this was all about.

The bus stop was deserted, apart from three Year Elevens puffing on vapes behind the shelter. Ramona and Lilah sat on the red metal seat inside.

'Now then, are you going to tell me what's happened, or are we going to sit here all night?' Ramona sounded like Tilly when she wanted to get the bottom of something.

Lilah let out a shuddery sigh, then seemed to recover herself. 'I can tell you one thing. I won't need you to be my alibi, after all. I wouldn't go out with Jamie rotten Tate if he was the last boy in the universe.'

'Did he ask you out, then?'

'Yes. No. Well sort of. He said there was a film he wanted to see, and he might ask me if I wanted to go with him, next weekend.'

'Right, so he said he might ask you out, but he didn't actually do it?'

'What I *said*.' Lilah looked at Ramona. 'Soz.'

'It's cool. So...?' Obviously, this vague date thing wasn't why Lilah was in such a state.

'He grabbed my hand at break this morning. He was laughing, mucking about. We both were. Then we ran across the field, and round the back of the gym, and he... we kissed, like, couple of times, you know...'

'Ah.'

'What's that mean, *ah*?'

'We saw you both coming back. I was with Mila and that lot. Everybody guessed you'd gone round there for a snog.'

Ramona expected Lilah to be appalled, or at least annoyed. Instead, she said, 'So what? The whole school probably knows by now, because Jamie's told them. Plus, he exaggerated the whole thing, made out we did other stuff, which is *so* not true. He went right back and told all his mates and they must have told all *their* mates, because I've been made fun of *all* afternoon. Even in Maths for Dummies, and you know what Mrs Boyle's like for talking in class.'

'Don't call it Maths for Dummies. It's a different set, that's all.'

'Yes, for people like me who are hopeless as hell at bloody maths.' Lilah bit her thumbnail. 'Anyway, we aren't talking about maths. We're talking about me being called a tramp and all horrible stuff. By *girls*, not only the boys.'

This was new territory. Ramona had no idea what to say that would help. 'It was only a snog, wasn't it?'

'Ramona!' Lilah's eyes were round with horror.

'Okay, sorry. Well, I don't know what everyone's so excited about, then.'

Privately, she thought twelve-going-on-thirteen was too young to be snogging anyway. At least, it would be for her. Even so, she wanted to ask Lilah what it was like kissing a boy for the first time, but now was not the moment.

'I don't know either. It's all so *juvenile*. It was just a stupid snog and it wasn't even that great. But why did he have to kiss and tell? Why boast about it and get practically the whole school on my back? It was meant to be our secret.' Lilah looked close to tears again.

'Did he say it was a secret?'

'Yes! I made him promise he wouldn't tell anyone and he said he wouldn't.'

Which wasn't quite the same thing, Ramona thought.

She nodded wisely, although she didn't feel wise at all. 'That's different, then. That's really bad, breaking a promise.'

'Well, that's it. I can't come to school tomorrow now everyone's talking about me.'

'Firstly, it won't be everyone. It'll only be kids in our year...'

'Oh, thanks. A great help you are.'

'... and secondly, like you said, it's not that big a deal. It'll have been forgotten by tomorrow. Anyway, you can't not come to school. You'll miss the revision sessions.'

And I need you to be there.

Another bus to Charnley Acre had gone by. Ramona really wanted to get on the next one. Empty or not, Number One The Pasture was her place of refuge. Besides, supposing this turned out to be the day Tilly was brought home, and she wasn't there to greet her? The thought caused her to feel all panicky inside.

Eventually, she persuaded Lilah to go home, have her tea, and forget all about Jamie and dating and snogging, and try to put the taunting into perspective.

'Walk into class tomorrow with your head held high. Look them in the eye and it'll be fine.'

'Okay. You're right. I'll go home in a minute,' Lilah said. 'Make sure you're there tomorrow, though. I can't face it without you. Don't let me down.'

Ramona smiled. 'As if.'

The kids with the vapes had wandered off, leaving wisps of smoke curling around the glass of the shelter and a fruity smell in the air. Lilah waited with Ramona until the next Charnley Acre bus arrived, then set off on her walk home. Ramona gave her a cheery wave from the bus window as they passed.

Lilah seemed fine at school the next morning; a bit subdued, but otherwise normal. Ramona was pleased she'd put yesterday's drama behind her. The trouble was, Ramona hadn't been able to do the same. Wasn't there enough misery in the world without overheated adolescents like Jamie Tate causing more? Her friend had been really upset yesterday, and it wasn't fair.

Lilah maybe okay morning, but she'd definitely not been okay last night. Her texts had been all angst and worry and they'd only stopped pinging through at ten o'clock when Ramona, her eyes drooping with tiredness, had written, kindly, that she had to go to sleep now, if that was okay.

She and Lilah were in the same lessons all morning, which was useful because it meant Ramona could keep an eye on her. Nobody teased Lilah or called her names in Ramona's hearing, but if they had, she had an idea Lilah was ready to give back as good as she got.

At lunch break Ramona had books to return to the library. Lilah said she'd stay behind in the refectory in case the dinner ladies doled out leftover chips, so Ramona was alone when she came face-to-face with Jamie, also alone, on the concrete path crossing the campus. Ramona stared long and hard at him, hoping to embarrass him. But no; he kind of smiled – no, *smirked* – at the ground as he passed her.

Ramona's sense of injustice reared up like a tidal wave. Adrenaline coursed through her, and before she could think what she was doing, she'd swung round, dropped her rucksack on the ground and in one swift movement made a grab for Jamie's bag which was dangling from his hand.

The weight of it took her by surprise, weight which worked well in her favour as she heaved up the bag and swung it at his head, scoring a direct hit. His eyes met hers in a flash of shock and confusion before he staggered sideways and fell onto the concrete. There was an *ooofff* sound as the breath rushed out of him.

'Shit! *Shit!*' He rolled over, looking up at Ramona in sheer disbelief. He levered himself up, resting on one elbow. 'What d'you do that for?'

He began to stagger to his feet. A bead of blood appeared on the right side of his chin; it must have come into direct contact with the path. Before he could stand upright, Ramona kicked out with all her strength, the toe of her leather shoe crunching against Jamie's kneecap. He yelped in pain. She kicked again, landing a blow on his shin. The rage was a glorious relief after weeks of restraint; weeks of holding on and keeping herself under strict control, in front of everyone, all the time. It rushed straight to her head, like the vodka cocktails Lilah had purloined from home last Christmas.

'You know what it's for! Now, go and tell all your mates you got beaten up by a girl! *If* you dare.'

She looked back only once as she walked away. He was sitting on the bank beside the path, rubbing his knee and swigging from a bottle of water. He'd be okay, a few bruises, that was all. And of course, he wouldn't tell.

Lilah must have realised that Jamie was missing that afternoon and all the following day, but she didn't mention it, and neither did Ramona. There was a stomach-clenching moment when one of the boys from their class tapped Ramona on the shoulder in the corridor and told her that 'Groper' was looking for her. But it was okay, because when she doubled back to the form room there were two boys and another girl already gathered round Mr Roper's desk and he was handing out duties for Thursday's open evening for prospective parents and pupils.

'It's a privilege to be chosen,' he said, his eyes swivelling across four doubtful faces. 'I expect you to be your best, most helpful selves on Thursday. In full uniform, clean and ironed, please. Although–' he winked '–you'll earn a quid for every child you can put off applying. The school's well over-subscribed.' Everyone laughed politely.

Those helping on open evening could either stay on straight after school, in which case a 'light meal' would be provided, or go home and come back at four-thirty. Ramona didn't have a choice. By the time she'd got all the way home to Charnley Acre, it would be time to get the bus straight back again. Well, a free tea wouldn't go amiss. She wasn't sure about the ironing part, though. After the first week of living alone, she'd stopped ironing and hung her clothes up straight from the machine, giving them a good shake instead.

Being at school after hours meant that parents or carers had to sign a permission slip, but Tilly's signature was an easy one, so that was no problem. Ramona relented, and ran the iron over a clean shirt and an almost-clean skirt on Wednesday evening. She was rather looking forward to being on meet-and-greet duty, despite the mild inconvenience of not getting home until eight.

On Thursday, Ramona went to the toilets after last lesson to wash her face, brush her hair, and check that she looked reasonably presentable. She even gave her shoes a buff with a wad of screwed-up toilet paper before joining the other helpers who were gathered at two tables in a corner of the refectory. Ham, cheese, and slices of cold pizza were set out on plates, along with lettuce, tomatoes and a pile of bread and butter, cut into floppy triangles. There was also a large metal tray of cold sponge pudding and a jug of custard, both of which Ramona recognised from lunchtime.

'Nothing cooked,' announced the dinner lady in charge. 'We don't want the place smelling of chip fat when the parents come round.'

Cold or not, the food was tasty – and free. Ramona's stomach felt pleasantly full as she took up her allotted position at the end of the lower corridor, ready to direct the visitors to the art room, the science labs, the music block, and the gym.

Simon, a gangly, sandy-haired boy from her class, was positioned on the opposite side of the corridor. He leant nonchalantly against the wall, chewing gum. The tip of a vape could clearly be seen poking from his trouser pocket.

'I'd get rid of that if I were you, in case the head comes along.' Ramona said helpfully. She meant the gum, not the vape. Best to pretend she hadn't seen that.

'Oh, you would, would ya?'

He chewed all the harder, grinding his jaw in a most unappealing way. Ramona averted her eyes. Why Mr Roper had picked Simon Cartwright for this evening's duties she had no idea. Unless he'd gone down the register with a pin.

'Yes, I would,' she said.

'Wasn't meant to be a question. You're a strange one, you are.' He shook his head.

Strange? Was she? Usually, she'd ignore a comment like that. Now, it was as if the world had been photoshopped, bringing it into razor-edged focus. She could pinpoint the moment it happened. It was just after she'd let her anger and frustration out of its cage and taken it out on Jamie.

Ramona stood in the empty corridor – empty apart from the gum-chewer – and felt her heart jolt with sadness and longing.

Longing for Tilly to come home and everything to go back to how it was before.

She thought about Tilly taking her to nursery, then to school, day in, day out, year in, year out, until Ramona insisted she was old enough for the school bus. Tilly had a car in those days, a battered old red one, its wheels permanently caked in mud from the field where it stood. Sometimes they'd give other children a lift home, even if it wasn't in the direction they were going. Ramona could see Tilly now, holding the back door of the car open and shooing them inside. *Shove up you three, that's it! Room for one more as long as it's a little one!* Then off they'd go, zipping along the road and zooming round the bends in the country lanes, making everyone shriek with laughter. It had seemed safe, though, always. She'd always felt safe in Tilly's hands.

She wasn't so sure she felt safe any more.

At the far end of the corridor, the double doors of the main hall were flung open and a swarm of nine-year-olds and adults emerged from the head's introductory talk. Ramona straightened her shoulders and arranged her expression into one of friendly politeness. Out of the corner of her eye, she saw Simon give a big sigh before he spat out the gum and pressed it with his thumb onto the wooden frame of the noticeboard behind him. What on earth did Lilah see in boys of their age? Most of them smelt of chewing gum and feet, if not worse.

'This way to the art room, then it's left and up the short staircase and follow the signs.'

'The gym display starts at half past five. The end door, then straight across the grass.'

Direction followed direction, smile followed smile, until Ramona's face ached with the effort. One of the fathers – she assumed he was the father of the boy with him – stopped to ask her how she liked the school, and were her parents pleased with her progress? She hadn't expected to be asked those sorts of questions. Yes, she told him, raising her chin. It was an excellent school, she hated the holidays when the school was shut, and her parents were *very proud indeed* of how well she was doing. The father widened his eyes at her, struggled with his mouth a bit, then said, 'Thank you.' The boy collapsed into laughter. Ramona couldn't see what was so funny. It was part of her job to sell the school, wasn't it? There was no point in doing a job if you didn't take it seriously.

Half an hour went by, quite slowly. Simon raised his eyes at her and even grinned, in a bored sort of way, before he gave up attempting to look efficient, folded himself against the wall like a sack of potatoes, and unwrapped another piece of chewing gum.

'Wanna bit?' He waved the packet.

Ramona smiled and shook her head. The corridor was almost empty now. A low-level buzz could be heard from the art room. Footsteps sounded faintly through the ceiling, tapping along the wooden floor of the upper corridor. The outside door, hidden from view, began to squeal as it opened and shut; the gym display must be over.

'Stand by your bunks,' Simon said, addressing the space in front of him rather than Ramona.

'It's tea in the hall and meet the teachers now, isn't it?'

A slim woman with smooth, honey-coloured hair addressed Ramona in a friendly voice. Her face was carefully made up, and her short black dress and heeled sandals looked expensive. Ramona wondered whether she'd dressed up specially for the open evening or if she always looked that smart. The girl by her side had the same colour hair. She wore a cute pink dress and white trainers without a single mark on them.

'You know it is. It's on the programme.' A broad-shouldered, dark-haired man cast his gaze over Ramona, then took the woman's elbow and steered her away, the girl trailing behind.

Ramona blinked, twice, in case her eyes were deceiving her. They weren't. The man had kept his back to Ramona, but she'd heard his voice. And now, as she looked along the corridor after them, he glanced behind, presumably to check that the girl – his daughter? – was following, and Ramona caught a full view of his face.

It was Ethan.

CHAPTER 18

She might not have been his wife or girlfriend, or the girl his daughter. The woman in the black dress could have been his sister, although they looked nothing like each other, one being so fair and the other so dark. She could have been his cousin, or some other relative – although Ramona couldn't immediately think of one. She could have been his next-door-neighbour, or simply a friend he'd given a lift to, and he'd gone into the school with her and her daughter instead of waiting outside in the car or coming back later to pick them up.

These thoughts buzzed manically around Ramona's mind like an angry wasp trapped in a jam jar. Even if she wasn't consciously thinking them, the thoughts were still there, banging on the glass, demanding attention. But what was she supposed to do, apart from going to Cloud Cottage and telling Emily about it?

If Emily came out with some perfectly reasonable explanation – cue, the sister/cousin/neighbour/friend scenario – then that would be fine, but in a way not fine, because it would make Ramona seem like a sneak and a troublemaker. The other possibility, in which Emily knew nothing about the woman and the child and would be shocked and upset, was a hundred times worse. She might even cry, and Ramona wasn't sure she could cope with that, knowing it was all her fault.

And yet, didn't Emily deserve to know if Ethan was a fake and had been betraying her all along? Emily was her friend. She'd been so lovely to Ramona, helped her survive these past weeks, although she didn't know it. Wasn't it kinder to tell her what she'd seen and let her make up her own mind about it?

The fact that none of this was any of Ramona's business, as she kept reminding herself, didn't make the decision any easier. It was *so* confusing.

She could ask Lilah. She was loads better at this sort of thing because she read the right magazines. But then it would mean telling her about Emily, and Cloud Cottage, and it would all come out about the lies she'd told and the life she'd invented for herself in order to shield herself from the people in authority and to have a grown-up friend like Emily, somebody she could rely on in a crisis, should there ever be one.

Tilly, through no fault of her own, had left a huge space in Ramona's life. A space that Emily had filled – well, partly. Several times, Ramona had been tempted to tell her the whole story. But, as always, the nightmare thoughts about the social people, the home for unwanted children, and, most importantly, the thought of letting Tilly down, had stopped her. There was only so far a friend was prepared to go before their conscience forced them into doing 'the right thing', even if it turned out it was the wrong thing, in the end.

So, no, she couldn't ask Lilah's advice, and neither she couldn't risk upsetting Emily and losing her friendship by telling tales about her boyfriend.

On the day school broke up for the summer holiday, Ramona and Lilah waited at Ramona's bus stop. It was only a quarter to three – they'd been let out early. The school grounds virtually tremored like pavements in a heatwave under the weight of sheer exuberance. A group of leavers were flinging sweatshirts, PE shorts, and science overalls into the trees and up the wire fence, where they caught and hung there like washing blown off a line in a hurricane. The girls were all tearful hugs, the boys play-fighting and yelling at each other for no particular reason. A few couples were snogging, not caring who saw.

'Do you wish that was us and this was our last day of school?' Lilah asked.

'No, I don't.' Ramona screwed up her forehead and looked at Lilah, surprised.

'I do. Instead of that, we've got four more whole years!' She sighed theatrically.

'Six, if you count sixth form.'

'Trust you to look on the bright side.' Lilah lifted her eyes. 'Still, we're free now. Let's make the most of it.' She grabbed hold of the bus stop pole and shimmied down it like a pole dancer. 'I want to *do* something, not just go home. Hey, shall I come with you, back to your house? Go on, it'll be a laugh.'

'To my house? Why?'

'Dunno, I just fancied it for a change. Not a problem, is it?'

Ramona's mouth had gone dry. 'No, it's not a problem. You'll have to get the bus all the way back home again, though.'

'So what?'

There was no answer to that.

Five minutes later, Ramona and Lilah pressed onto the bus with a horde of other kids and found seats together at the back. Resigned now, Ramona wondered glumly what the outcome of this diversion from the norm would be.

Whatever will be will be, sang Tilly in Ramona's head.

'Lilah, if you knew somebody's boyfriend was cheating on them, would you tell them, even if you weren't completely certain?' Ramona asked, as the bus left the main road and chugged towards Charnley Acre and its surrounds.

Lilah looked at her. 'Yeah, too right I would. If it was me, I'd want to know. Where's that come from, anyway?'

'It was in a book I was reading, that's all. I only wondered.' Ramona shrugged.

'So, did the person in the book tell the person with the boyfriend?'

'I haven't got to that bit yet.' Ramona pressed the bell. 'This is our stop.'

Number One The Pasture seemed to Ramona to be holding its breath as the two girls approached.

'Is Tilly out, then?' Lilah looked around as they stood in the kitchen. 'Or is she upstairs?'

Ramona cocked her head to one side, pretending to be listening for signs of movement.

'Out, definitely. Do you want cake or biscuits?'

'Crisps?'

'Mm, no, sorry. I forgot when I went... did the online shop for Tilly.'

'No prob. What are the cakes and biscuits?'

Ramona looked in the cupboard, knowing full well what she'd find there. 'Currant cakes, home-made. I made them myself. The biscuits are only Rich Tea fingers.'

'Currant cakes, then. Have you got any juice? Orange, or pineapple?' Lilah had the larder door open.

'Orange squash, that's all.' The cheap stuff. 'Or we could have tea?'

'Squash will do, thanks.'

Ramona couldn't help noticing how Lilah's nose wrinkled at the sight of the label on the bottle.

'There isn't much in your larder,' Lilah observed, eating her cake standing up and dropping crumbs on the floor. She opened the fridge and pulled a face at the almost-empty shelves. 'You must have forgotten more than the crisps. I hope for your sake your gran's gone shopping.'

'Don't be so nosey.' Ramona came behind her and shut the fridge door. 'What shall we do now?'

'Whatever. Let's go up to your room.'

Taking another cake each from the tin, they went upstairs. Ramona's bedroom, being right under the eaves, was hot and stuffy. She thought it best not to leave any windows open while she was out. She undid the catch and lifted up the bottom section of the sash window as far as it would go. Still hot, she peeled off her sweatshirt. As she did so, the hem of her white shirt rose with it, revealing her midriff.

'Jeesus!' Lilah said. 'You're *so* skinny! Have you been dieting and not told me?'

Ramona tugged the shirt down again. 'I've been careful what I eat.'

She leaned on the sill of the open window, facing Lilah who'd sat down on the bed. 'Shall we play a computer game? Or we could watch telly downstairs?'

But Lilah wasn't finished with the subject of Ramona's slimmed-down look. Trust her to notice when Ramona hadn't. Well, maybe she had noticed her school skirt hung lower down on her hips now and her jeans were roomier in the waist than before, but she hadn't given it serious thought. Okay, she hadn't been eating as much fresh meat and fish, partly because of the cost, but also because she didn't know how to make the kinds of dinners Tilly made. And she could make a cheap white loaf last a week if she used the end up for toast. But the situation was only temporary, and it wasn't as if she'd collapsed from malnutrition. In fact, she felt as fit and healthy as ever; a bit more tired perhaps, but that was nothing.

Lilah was lifting her own shirt, gazing critically at the exposed pale flesh. 'Do you think I need to lose a few pounds, too?'

'Of course not. You're really thin... slim, I mean.'

'But not as thin as you.' Lilah looked Ramona right in the eye. 'You are okay, aren't you? I mean, it's cool if you lost weight with healthy eating and that, but you didn't actually need to. Did somebody say something at school? Call you fat or anything?'

'No, they didn't. Please can we not talk about it any more?'

'Well, all right, but just be careful, that's all.'

Lilah was looking around the room, giving it a virtual tour of inspection. She had a look of mistrust about her. Lilah might show a devil-may-care face to the world, but she was nobody's fool. Ramona closed her eyes for a second and took a deep breath. When she opened them again, Lilah was holding up two mugs and an empty cereal bowl she must have found on the floor beside the bed. Well, it was so hard to keep up when you had to do everything yourself.

'These must've been here for ages. The milk's all gone sour. Slummy or what?' Lilah laughed, then seeing Ramona's face, fell serious.

'Sorry, I didn't mean that. It's a surprise, that's all. You're not like this.'

Like what? She didn't need to explain. The two girls looked at each other.

'Ramona, what's going on?'

'Nothing's going on.' Ramona tried to laugh. It didn't work.

Lilah kept her gaze on Ramona. Her eyes had a softness about them that almost made Ramona cry.

'Okay,' she said at last. 'Okay, I'll tell you.'

They sat together on the wooden bench which leaned drunkenly against the shed in the back garden, facing the pointed arches of bamboo canes entwined with rampant greenery. Among the chaos of vegetable leaves and weeds, shrunken bean-pods hung, black and worm-like. Sober heads of roses drooped, mourning the loss of the brown petals at their feet. Grass and dandelions sprouted between the flagstones of the path, and the fence was hardly visible under its mantle of flowering bindweed.

'I thought I was your bestie. I thought you trusted me,' Lilah said.

'You are, and I do. But if I'd told you, it would have changed everything. You'd have asked questions. You'd have made me stop believing.'

'Believing Tilly got sent to Seaview House by mistake, and she's okay and she's just waiting for them to send her home? Is that what you mean?'

Ramona's insides jolted. It sounded... unrealistic, coming from Lilah. Probably because it was the first time she'd heard it said out loud. Had she got it wrong about Tilly? Could she really have imagined what was going on so vividly it had become the truth?

But it was the only truth she had.

She swallowed. 'Yes, that's what I mean,' she said quietly.

'So, what are we going to do?' Lilah asked.

'*We*? How d'you mean?'

'Well, I'm not leaving you here on your own for starters. Pack some stuff and we'll go back to mine.'

Ramona stood up. The bench tilted upwards at one end, like an unbalanced see-saw. She faced Lilah.

'You *see*? It's already happening. Now you know, everything's changed! It's all... *wrong*! I had it all straight in my head, and now it's got muddled up!'

She turned and bolted inside, shutting the back door after her.

Moments later, Lilah came after her. Too much to hope that she'd taken the hint and gone home.

'I s'pose,' Lilah said gently, to Ramona's back, 'that what you said is sort of possible. They do make mistakes in hospitals. You see it on telly and in the papers all the time. Hundreds of mistakes, ginormous ones.'

Ramona turned from facing the kitchen sink to see Lilah's eyes wide and bright and eager. She laughed. It relieved the tension a bit.

'You don't mean that.'

Lilah laughed, too. 'P'raps not *quite* that many mistakes. You're right about not being allowed to stay here on your own, though. I know that from my dad. He deals with all sorts, being a police officer.'

'Which is why,' Ramona said, 'you can't tell anyone. Not your mum, and especially not your dad. I won't let them take me away, and you're not to let them either. *Please*, Lilah.'

Ramona's stomach was clenched tight with nerves. She had to persuade Lilah to keep her secret. *Had* to. Otherwise, she was doomed. Besides, miraculously, the muddle in her head had unravelled itself and there was her belief, shiny and intact. Tilly *would* come home, very soon. And it would be like none of this had ever happened.

'Please?' The word came out as a whisper.

'Okay,' Lilah said eventually. 'Okay. But just for now, right?'

'Right.'

'But if you're in any kind of trouble, you'll come straight to me. Yes?'

Ramona nodded.

Later, she went with Lilah to the bus stop; there was a bus due at twenty past five. They'd eaten the last of the currant cakes, washed down with mugs of tea, then they'd watched telly, mostly in silence, but it felt comfortable.

Ramona turned down Lilah's invitation to go home with her for dinner, making her swear she wouldn't say a word about Ramona's situation. The idea of being given dinner was tempting, but she felt too wired to relax and be sociable in somebody else's house. At the same time, she felt spaced out with tiredness. All she wanted to do was make herself beans on toast then curl up with more telly until it was a reasonable time to go to bed.

'Come for your dinner tomorrow, then,' Lilah had said, as the bus appeared. 'We could go somewhere in the day, if you like? Our first day of freedom!'

Ramona thought for a moment. 'Could we go to Cliffhaven? There's something I need to do.'

They gazed at Seaview House from the opposite side of the road, standing on the grass beyond the road itself. Behind them, facing the sea, were benches and a shelter for people to sit and take in the view, and a wire fence guarding the cliff edge. In front of them, the traffic whizzed by.

'Look, why don't we just go in and ask to see her? That's why we've come, isn't it?' Lilah said. She was fed up with standing about, just looking, Ramona could tell.

'No, of course not! I told you, I can't let anyone know. About me, I mean. They'll ask questions and then everyone'll go nuts and...'

Oh, but she wanted to see Tilly *so* much, she could hardly bear being so close to her, yet so far apart! Surely Lilah understood.

She did. 'Yeah, see your point. So, it's just the card then. Which we could have posted, by the way.'

'It's not the same,' Ramona said. 'I thought I'd explained. I need to know it's arrived safely. I need to do this for Tilly.'

'Okay, then. Let's go in and hand it in. You'll have me. It'll be all right. Be brave.'

'It's not a matter of being brave. It's a matter of self-preservation.'

'Is it?'

'Yes, it is. I have to stick to the plan. Are you coming with me to deliver this, or stopping here?'

Ramona held up the pink envelope she'd carried in her hand for the whole of the bus ride from Charnley Acre, through Cliffhaven town centre, and all the way along the seafront. The corners had got a bit creased from being held, but she hadn't wanted to put it in her backpack where she couldn't see it.

'I'm coming.'

'Okay, but we have to be quick. No dilly-dallying.'

'*Dilly-dallying*? I don't know where you get some of your words.'

As soon as there was a gap in the traffic they sprinted across the road, straight over the pavement, in through the open black iron gates, and along the path to the dusty, black-painted front door of Seaview House. Ramona posted the card through the brass letterbox which was patched with fingerprints, then they turned and sprinted back again, stopping breathlessly by the shelter.

Lilah went to sit down in the empty shelter, but Ramona tugged her away. Now she'd been right up to the door of the nursing home, it seemed important to be out of sight of it.

They walked back towards the town, Ramona conjuring up a picture in her mind of a nurse or care assistant picking up the pink envelope and taking it to Tilly. Of course, Tilly would know without opening it who it was from. When she did open it, she'd find the prettiest picture of a country garden with a rose bower, and inside she would read the words in Ramona's best handwriting: *Dear Mrs Donnelly, I hope you get Well Soon. Best Wishes.*

She'd reached out to Tilly, and even if Tilly couldn't reach out to her, it was better than nothing. Tilly would know Ramona was thinking about her. The card was like a secret sign, a coded message.

A small ember of satisfaction glowed inside her.

'Aren't you going to put your lovely card up on your locker, where you can see it?' the girl – Karen, that's her name isn't it? – asks.

Karen has taken the card out of the pink envelope for her. Tilly's all fingers and thumbs these days. Not that the card is for her. It can't be, because it says *get well soon* and she's as fit as a flea. A bit fuzzy and forgetful sometimes, but otherwise as chirpy as a cricket.

'Look,' Karen says, 'it's got your name in it. Isn't that nice of somebody to have sent it? A pity they forgot to put their own name, but perhaps you know who it's from?'

Tilly smiles. She likes Karen. She's the one who tells Tilly she has a beautiful complexion and looks nothing like her age. If that isn't Tilly's name in the card, where Karen's finger is pointing, there must be somebody else here with the same name. Donnelly isn't an unusual name, is it? She lets Karen stand the card on top of her locker anyway, and goes back to the window, leaning on the stick they gave her. She doesn't need the damn thing. It gets in the way. She only uses it to please them.

She stands close to the window and peers out, the fingertips of one hand resting on the glass. It feels cold to the touch. Before she got interrupted with the card that was meant for someone else, she'd been looking at the sea when she'd seen two girls standing on the grass across the road. They were talking to one another and one of them was holding something pink; Tilly couldn't see what from this distance.

As she'd watched them, that funny feeling had come back, the one where there was something in her stupid head, on the tip of her useless tongue. Something she needs to say. Only she can't quite catch hold of it, no matter how hard she tries. The words, whatever they are, hold an idea, a very special thought. The thought torments her, and just when she thinks she's close to it, it slips out of her grasp again like a wet fish.

But, oh, she does need to tell somebody! That much she knows.

She turns a half-circle, slowly because her leg doesn't want to go where she wants it to these days, ready to ask Karen about the girls. But Karen's gone, and when Tilly turns back to the window, the girls have gone, too.

Later, after she's had her lunch in the dining room with a lot of old people – some of them look respectable; others, well, she'd rather not think about them – she remembers the girls on the grass again.

'I would very much like to go out,' she says to the young man who comes to clear away the plates. '*Very* much.'

She's sitting in the lounge when Karen comes with a coat for her and says something about sea air.

The traffic seems very loud, up close. Now she hears the awful noise of it, Tilly knows she's been out here before, but she's not sure she likes it.

'Are we going shopping?' she says to Karen. 'I do hope so because I've got to get some of that breakfast stuff – what's it called?'

Karen has a tight hold of her arm. Too tight, but Tilly doesn't say anything. Karen looks past Tilly at the nice young man who has her other arm. How's she supposed to move about with these two hanging on?

'Breakfast stuff? Do you mean cereal?' Karen says. 'You don't need cereal. There's plenty.'

'No, no.' Tilly tries to break free from the restraining hands. 'The one *she* likes. We haven't got any. I've got to get the right one. Will you help me find it? Where's my shopping bag?'

'Come on, Tilly,' the young man says. 'Let's get across this road and we'll sit on a seat and watch the sea.'

Tilly harrumphs. 'I can see it perfectly well from my window, thank you very much.'

But they're through the cars, over the pavement, and onto the grass on the other side now, and Tilly remembers the girls again. The smaller one with the straight brown hair in particular.

'Where are they? Where've they gone?' She looks up and down.

Nobody answers her. Nobody ever does, these days, not even when she's saying something important.

She finds herself being steered to a seat, and there she sits with the wind in her hair, wearing somebody else's coat. Karen sits beside her and the young man sits next to Karen. He's smoking a cigarette.

'You know that's very bad for you,' Tilly scolds. 'You ought to pack it in.'

He laughs. 'You're absolutely right there, Mrs Donnelly.'

'Shall I tell you a secret?' Tilly leans conspiratorially towards the pair of them. 'I do enjoy a cheroot. I could have one now, only I don't seem to have them with me. Have you got them? Have you got my cheroots?'

'Does she really smoke cheroots?' the young man says to Karen.

And Karen says, 'No idea,' at the same as Tilly says, 'Yes, I do. What of it?'

'She's not so far gone, is she?' Tilly hears the young man say.

'Nope, she makes a lot of sense, at times,' Karen says. 'She makes me laugh.'

Tilly smiles and looks at the sea. She wonders who they're talking about.

CHAPTER 20

On Monday morning, Emily sat at her desk in the open-plan office of the *Cliffhaven News* and checked her mobile phone. There was no message from Ramona. It seemed strange that she should have ignored the text Emily sent yesterday. School had finished for the summer holiday so she wouldn't have homework, but she was such a polite child that Emily couldn't believe she'd taken what she needed and disappeared without another word.

Perhaps she simply hadn't seen the message – she wasn't glued to her phone as Emily imagined most girls of her age were. She'd be too busy planning her holidays and having fun amid that large, boisterous family of hers. And rightly, too. Emily's text had expressed hope that Ramona's exams had gone well, and said she'd be welcome at Cloud Cottage whenever she liked; that was all. It hadn't actually needed a reply and she was probably wrong to have expected one.

She'd grown used to seeing Ramona sitting at the table, writing away, and chewing the end of her biro when she was thinking hard. Sometimes she'd be so engrossed that she wouldn't hear Emily come into the room. Then she'd see a drink and slice of cake arrive on the table, and her solemn little face would be transformed by the most engaging smile.

The truth was, Emily missed her.

She missed Ethan, too. The conference would be over by now, and he'd be somewhere unspecified in Yorkshire, catching up with his mates, mates Emily knew nothing about and had never warranted a mention before, as far as she could remember.

But that was Ethan. He'd never been very forthcoming on the details of his personal history, and she'd been shown only the vaguest picture of his life before they met. It hadn't seemed to matter before. Whether or not it mattered now was questionable. It seemed she would only know the answer to that when he came back.

She'd decided to use the space Ethan had put between them to examine her true feelings for him, but each time she tried, her mind wandered off and she found herself re-living the happy times, the loving times, the times when his words and kisses spoke of promise and anticipation.

The times when he'd said he loved her and she'd said it back, with no doubt in her mind, or her heart, whatsoever. But now... well, somehow it seemed a lot more complicated than that.

Emily turned her attention back to a feature she was writing about a residents' protest. A crumbling Victorian mansion in Cliffhaven had been earmarked to be developed and turned a women's refuge, and the horrified owners of the detached houses in the leafy avenue were busily writing to the *Letters* page of the paper and holding up polite banners on the steps of the council offices. On the day Emily had interviewed some of the protestors, she'd stood outside the mansion, gazing up at the ornate chimneys rising above the high, graffitied brick wall that surrounded the property while the photographer poked his lens through the barbed wire covering the entrance. The planned alterations and updating would mean the house would be able to accommodate at least ten women and their children.

Emily had nodded understandingly as she'd recorded the protestors' concerns, while all the while her heart was cheering the planning application all to the way to rip-roaring success.

'Who's coming bowling later? Pizza afterwards.' Kelly, an advertising assistant, swung round in her chair and addressed the office in general.

The bowling alley wasn't large and was desperate for a bit of refurbishing, but it had a bar with friendly staff and was a stone's throw from the *Cliffhaven News* building, making it a popular early-evening gathering place. The cheap and cheerful Italian restaurant next door added to the attraction.

There were several 'yeses', Emily's not among them.

'Emily?'

'I don't think so, thanks.'

'Why's that, then?' Andy, a freelance reporter, shot her a disappointed look from the opposite desk. 'Not working tonight are you?'

'I'm hoping not. I don't fancy it, that's all.'

Not so long ago, she'd hardly missed a chance to socialise. Whether there'd been a current boyfriend or not, she'd always be going somewhere, doing something. Laura used to complain, in a non-serious way, that she could never get hold of her. These days, Emily just looked forward to getting home to Cloud Cottage.

She gazed at her reflection in the darkened computer screen. Perhaps she was getting old.

Having edited and filed the final copy of the women's refuge piece, she left the office at half past four. That in itself was reason not to relent and join the others at the bowling alley, in case they thought she was being a misery; the general gravitation in its direction didn't begin until half five or six. But she didn't feel like going straight home either. Reaching the crossroads at the Charnley Acre end of the Cliffhaven road, she took a left instead of the usual right and drove up Charnley Hill to Spindlewood.

It wasn't until she reached the top of the drive and looked up at the silent house, its red brick frontage glowing somnolently in the afternoon sun, that she remembered: Laura and Clayton were away. They'd left yesterday for the cottage in the Lake District. They'd got engaged on their first holiday there and returned every summer once Laura's school, where she taught children with special needs, had broken up.

Emily stopped the car and got out, stretching her arms high above her head to release the tension from sitting at a keyboard all day. What a nuisance! Once the idea had come into her head, she'd been looking forward to a cup of tea and a natter with Laura. It was exactly what she needed, and now there was no prospect of that for at least a fortnight. Shaking her head at the pure selfishness of this thought, Emily climbed back into the car and drove off again.

Back at the crossroads at the bottom of Charnley Hill, she made an instant decision to drive home the long way round. Avoiding the high street, she took the road that twisted and turned around the northern edge of the village. Thin woodland and undulating farmland stretched away on either side. On Emily's left, the South Downs cast elongated blue shadows across the lower slopes. She drove slowly, past a row of ancient cottages and the entrance to a farm, enjoying the sweet scent of the air through the open window. Not that she had any choice but to drive slowly – the bus up ahead had come to a stop, and the road was so narrow was no room to pass safely. She pulled onto a patch of grass beside a fence surrounding a field of grazing sheep, switched off the engine and waited. She was in no hurry.

The bus doors closed with a pneumatic swish, and the bus moved on. Two people had alighted: a woman with a shopping basket, who turned towards the cottages – and Ramona.

Emily thrust her face closer to the windscreen. The girl she'd seen dashing along the grass verge had disappeared, but she hadn't been mistaken, she was sure of it.

Restarting the engine and manoeuvring the car closer to the fence, Emily got out. She looked around, but there was no sign of Ramona, nor were there any houses other than those few tiny cottages, and she hadn't gone in that direction. Beside the bus stop, the fields gave way to a dense thicket of trees and bushes. Ramona – if it *was* her and not a trick of Emily's imagination – had vanished amongst them.

Ramona, when pressed for an answer by Emily, had said she lived on the Meadowside estate. It made sense. The houses there, originally built by the council, were spacious enough to accommodate a large family. In which case, what was the girl doing here?

Emily walked on past the bus stop and there, between the trees, she could see the white walls and part of the roof of a house. It seemed like a small house; a cottage, really, not much bigger than the diminutive dwellings further along the road. Puzzled, Emily stepped further onto the grass verge beside a kind of entrance with a broken fence, and peered between the trees. She felt like a stalker, or at the very least somebody who should be minding their own business. But her concerns about Ramona's weight loss and her sometimes unkempt appearance began crowding in, conspiring with the unacknowledged phone text to propel Emily closer until she was virtually standing in the front garden of the cottage. Although, with no visible boundaries, it was hard to tell which was garden and which was field.

'Number One The Pasture' said the wooden sign, the gouged-out letters made indistinct by age. Emily hadn't realised there was a house here, and she'd driven by enough times. But you'd have to look closely to notice it. Judging by the number of windows, it looked to be no more than a two-up-and-two-down, or it had been originally – she could see some kind of extension on the back at ground level. The house obviously wasn't home to a police officer, his wife, and five children. And anyway, why would Ramona lie about living at Meadowside? And yet she must be inside. Where else could she have gone? There were no other buildings around, apart from a tumbledown shed way across the field. Was she visiting whoever lived here? Was the cottage even lived in at all? It had an air of melancholy about it, which the closed curtains only served to enhance.

Standing where she was, she must be in full view of anyone looking out of the windows, but Emily was too intrigued, too mystified, and too full of concern for Ramona to worry about that. She stepped up to the low-lintelled front door and banged the knocker, twice. There was no answer, and no sign of any movement from inside, but she knew what she'd seen, and she hadn't imagined it.

She stood back, arms folded, and gazed up at the windows. They gazed blankly back.

'Ramona? Ramona! It's me, Emily!'

Nothing. Where was she? What was she doing in there?

Emily knocked again, more firmly. She thought she detected a sound from inside. She put her ear to the door but all was silent. Short of attempting to break in – it hadn't quite come to that – there was nothing more she could do. She backed away from the door. Taking a last look at the cottage, she turned and went back to the car.

Once inside, she took her mobile phone from her bag and called Ramona's number. It went straight to voicemail. Emily sat with both hands on the steering wheel. What next? She could try Ramona's mobile again later, keep trying until she got an answer. Or she could come back here later, or tomorrow. The girl may be perfectly okay, and there could be an innocent explanation for why she was here, in this remote cottage, apparently hiding, although it was impossible to imagine what it might be.

Emily sat on for a few more minutes, deep in thought. She felt frustrated at her own failure and her concern for Ramona was gaining traction by the minute. But, for now, there was nothing to be gained by hanging about here. She started the car, grating the gears as she pulled out onto the road.

She'd only driven a short distance when she looked in the rear-view mirror and saw Ramona running down the middle of the road towards the car, waving her arms and mouthing 'Stop!'

CHAPTER 21

For some reason, Emily had insisted they go right back to Number One The Pasture. She'd reversed the car, with Ramona in it, really fast, her hands gripping the steering wheel, as if she was dead cross about something. Ramona would much rather have been taken to Cloud Cottage where she felt safe and where she could pretend everything was normal.

'I could come back with you,' she'd said, really quietly, so as not to make Emily crosser than she already was.

But Emily had just said, 'No' in a firm voice. Then her eyes had gone all soft and she hadn't seemed cross any more.

Ramona had not long been home from Lilah's house. She'd stopped off at the minimart nearby to pick up some supplies before she'd caught the bus. She and Lilah had been to Lewes today. A couple of girls from their class had been on the same bus, and all four of them had wandered round the shops and the stalls in the indoor market. They'd bought Diet Cokes and snacks, and sat on a seat on the bridge overlooking the river, having a laugh. Ramona had needed that, more than anything.

She hadn't needed any persuading to go back to Lilah's house for her tea. They'd eaten hard-boiled eggs, ham, salad and oven chips with Lilah's mum, Sophie and Tim – the rest of the family were out. When Lilah's mum had asked, as she always did, she'd had to go through the charade of pretending Tilly had given her permission to stay out as long as she liked. But the untruth was necessary, and she'd got so used to telling it that it didn't feel so much like a lie any more.

It had been a good day, a day when she'd felt especially optimistic, as well as proud that she'd come so far on her own without anything awful happening. Keeping busy, having a giggle with her friends, had worked liked magic and she'd managed to keep Tilly – Emily, too, and Ethan – out of her mind for most of the time.

Back home, she'd been about to open the downstairs curtains – she tended to keep them closed when she was out, just in case – when she'd seen Emily standing in the front garden. She'd twitched the curtains shut again, her heart racing. Seconds later, she'd heard her name being called, and then came the knocking at the door. *Knock, knock, knock*, as if Emily had wanted to break the door down.

How had she found out where she lived? That in itself was bad enough, but did she also know Ramona was home alone? If so, how? The only person who knew her secret was Lilah, and she would never tell. She didn't even know Emily.

She'd felt panicky and sick as she'd backed away from the window, knocking against a chair as she did so. Clearly Emily wasn't leaving any time soon. What was she supposed to do? She could hardly open the door, say 'hi' and make out this was all totally normal when it obviously wasn't. But the thought of having to come up with another pack of lies or, even more daunting, tell the outright truth, had made her head feel like it was about to explode. There'd seemed no choice but to keep quiet and pretend she wasn't here. Pretend she wasn't *anywhere*.

As she'd stood in the gloom of the darkened room, the panicky feeling had changed into something else. Knowing Emily was right outside the door had given her the tiniest sensation of having been saved. Saved from what, she didn't know, because she was okay, wasn't she? She was doing just fine. She didn't need anyone apart from Tilly and if she had to wait a bit longer for her, she could cope with that.

And then, curiosity had taken over. She'd moved back to the window and peeped through the gap in the curtains. As she'd watched Emily hurrying away it had felt like the worst thing in the whole world. For a long moment, she hadn't been able to move; she'd hardly been able to breathe. And then something inside her had snapped, and her feet had carried her to the front door and out onto the lane.

Now, they stood in the kitchen, Emily's gaze sweeping across the sinkful of washing-up, the splodges of baked bean juice on the top of the stove, the soggy washing on the clothes horse and chair backs, and the sticky floor. She wished she'd taken Emily straight through to the living room where at least things looked right, apart from the dust on the tops of the furniture. But Emily didn't seem to want to move. She stood facing Ramona, looking her right in the eye, and Ramona had to make a big effort to look right back at her and not out of the window.

'Ramona, is this where you live?' Emily's voice was all soft. Not like her eyes, which were talking in another way altogether.

'Yes.'

'Where's your mother?'

'My mother died of a pulmonary embolism when I was three days and two hours old. A pulmonary embolism is a blood clot in the lung. I've read all about it.'

'Oh, Ramona...'

A small silence, then: 'What about your father, the policeman? Where is he?'

'I haven't got a father. Well, I have got one, otherwise I couldn't have been born, but I don't know who it is. It doesn't say on my birth certificate.'

'Who do you live with, then? Who takes care of you?'

'Tilly does. My mother was called Caroline, and Tilly was *her* mother.'

'So, Tilly's your grandmother and her name's Matilda Donnelly. Am I right?'

'Yes.'

'She brought you up?'

'Yes.'

'Ramona, you haven't got any brothers and sisters, have you?'

Emily's eyes had caught up with her voice now and gone all swishy.

'No, I haven't. Don't be sad, though, because it's all right.' Ramona smiled a bit. 'I'm very sorry I told you I lived at Meadowside and made up those people for you, but I had to. I didn't make them up completely, though. They are a real family. Just not my family.'

'*Why*, Ramona?'

She couldn't answer. The question was too big. It took up too much space. The words swam around in her brain, like tiny fish in a vast ocean.

'Never mind,' Emily said gently. 'Ramona, Tilly's not here, is she?'

'Would you like a cup of tea? I've got biscuits. Only Rich Tea, though...'

'Ramona.'

Ramona looked at the floor. Her eyes refused to stay on Emily's face any longer.

'Tilly's not here at the moment but I know where she is.'

'I think I do, too,' Emily said.

Ramona made herself look up again. She needed to explain. Things had gone too far for any more fairy stories.

'Yes. I heard you in the shop when I was waiting in the queue. You were talking about my Tilly. You said she'd fainted in the heat and the ambulance took her away. Or the man said, I don't remember now. That's how I knew she'd gone to the hospital when she didn't come home.' Ramona put her finger to her chin, tilting her head sideways, casting her mind back to a place that felt so very far away, but really wasn't. 'I didn't know for *totally* certain until I rang them up and pretended to be you, but I didn't say your name because I didn't know what it was then.' She gave Emily a serious look, because this *was* serious and Emily wasn't looking very happy. 'Don't worry, I wouldn't have given your name even if I had known what it was. That wouldn't have been right.'

Emily didn't speak for a minute. She had her hand over her mouth. She was thinking hard, Ramona could tell.

'I'm very sorry for pretending I was you. It was sneaky.'

And then Emily stopped thinking and gave a big grin. 'Actually, I'd call it ingenious.'

'Ingenious,' Ramona repeated. 'Yes, it was, wasn't it?'

Emily could tell by the look in Ramona's eye that she considered it a small victory to be able to tell her that Tilly wasn't in hospital now but in a nursing home called Seaview House. Her sparky independence, the sense of being in control of her own destiny, was still intact after all she'd been through, and Emily loved and admired her for it. And to have inveigled Emily into letting her come to Cloud Cottage because she recognised her in the library and decided she could trust her, well, who'd have thought? She'd certainly taken Emily in with her story about her big noisy family.

She'd heard the rest of the story while Ramona washed up and Emily dried – Ramona insisted on doing the washing. This was after Emily had worked out how to reignite the pilot light on the boiler and they'd had a cup of tea while they waited for the water to heat up.

'I don't suppose you know how to make the washing machine spin as well?' Ramona asked hopefully, eyeing the very wet sheets, towels, and clothes decorating the kitchen.

''Fraid not. It's more of a specialist job.'

'It doesn't matter. I'm sure I can find somebody who can do it before Tilly comes home.'

Ramona's unwavering optimism – not only about the washing machine – brought a tear to Emily's eye, and she had to turn away. In fact, she'd been hard pressed to hold it together since she learned the reason why Ramona had ploughed on alone once Tilly had been taken from her, and kept it all a secret.

Looking around, Emily took in the comfortable furnishings, the lined cotton curtains in bright, fresh colours, the polished brass door knobs, the bright copper coal scuttle on the hearth and the oak bookcase containing not only books and magazines but a sizeable collection of CDs, mostly opera. On top of the bookcase were two small packets of cheroots, one of them open, and a box of matches.

'Tilly's the opera fan, I take it?' Emily said. She didn't like to mention the cheroots. 'Sorry. I'm being nosey, aren't I?'

Ramona shrugged. 'No, you're not, you're just *interested*. Yes, she loves it. She likes to play it really loud, but it's okay because there's nobody to hear except the sheep.'

Emily smiled. The girl was like a breath of fresh air.

A silver-framed photo showing two people sat on the tiled mantelpiece. Emily recognised Matilda Donnelly – Tilly – from that day in the village shop, and a younger version of Ramona. She could hardly begin to imagine Tilly's pain at losing Caroline, her daughter, in such tragic circumstances. Looking at grandmother and granddaughter in the photo, their hair blowing in the wind as they stood on a beach somewhere, Emily recognised the same strength and determination in them both.

Ramona saw her looking. 'We were in Devon, on holiday. We stayed in a guest house. Tilly asked a man to take our photo. I was eight, I think. Or nine.'

'It's a great photo,' Emily said.

Ramona looked at the photo, then back at Emily.

'Why hasn't Tilly come home yet? Is it because the Seaview people haven't got round to it? I think that must be it.'

It was no good lying. Ramona deserved better than that.

'Tilly might not be quite as well as you think she is. She might not be well enough to come home at the moment.'

'Oh.' Ramona looked down at her feet, then back at Emily, narrowing her grey eyes. 'You don't know that for certain, though, do you?'

'No, I don't know for certain...'

'But you could find out, couldn't you? Emily, will you find out for me?'

'Of course.' Emily smiled. 'But let's get you home... to Cloud Cottage, I mean, and then I'm sure we can sort something out.'

She'd expected a protest when she told Ramona she was taking her back to Cloud Cottage. Instead, she'd simply nodded and said, 'Thank you.' Her look of relief had made Emily want to hug her, but as she'd taken a step towards her, the girl backed away. Emily took it as a warning that Ramona couldn't take too much all at once.

While Ramona was upstairs packing a bag, Emily went into

the living room, closed the door, and plugged in the landline phone. She listened to the message on the answer machine, and by the time Ramona had come down again, Glenda Robertson's name and number were safely tucked away on a slip of paper inside Emily's bag.

Emily told Ramona she wouldn't go to her office or out to interview anyone for a few days, at least. She might have to do some work at home, but it meant she wouldn't be leaving Ramona on her own. Ramona told Emily, quite plainly, that she'd be fine, and if Emily wanted to go to work then she should go. But Emily wouldn't hear of it.

'Nope. You're stuck with me whether you like it or not.' She'd laughed as she said it.

But Ramona did like it, a lot; she just didn't want to be a nuisance. She loved being at Cloud Cottage, too. It felt safe and familiar and cosy, especially the bedroom Emily put her in, which was so pretty and had a double bed in it – a whole double bed, just for her!

'I've never slept in a double bed before,' she'd said to Emily, when she'd taken Ramona upstairs to show her the room. 'Oh, except when I had chickenpox and got all hot and scratchy. Tilly put me in her bed so I'd keep cooler, and she slept in mine.'

'That was sensible,' Emily had said. 'I imagine chickenpox can be awfully scratchy. I never had it myself.'

'Well, you shouldn't go near anybody who's got it then,'

Ramona had said, 'because at your age it could be *very* dangerous.'

Emily seemed to find that funny; Ramona couldn't see why.

On Ramona's first full day at Cloud Cottage, they went to The Ginger Cat café in the village for lunch. Emily said they deserved a little treat. Ramona ate two poached eggs on two pieces of toast and wondered how long to leave it before she could remind Emily she was supposed to be finding out about Tilly. Then, as she was deciding whether she could manage a strawberry cupcake or whether an ice cream would be better, Emily's mobile phone rang and she snatched it up off the table and went and stood outside on the pavement to take the call. It must have been something really private, Ramona decided.

Perhaps it was Ethan. Her heart jumped at the thought. She'd almost forgotten about him, and what she'd seen at the school open evening.

When Emily came back and sat down again, her face looked serious. The call hadn't been from Ethan but something to do with Tilly. She had some news, she said. She'd tell Ramona all about it when they got home. Ramona didn't think she could wait that long and she asked Emily if she would please tell her, now. Emily's face went from serious to serious-doubtful. She ordered a coffee for herself, but nothing for Ramona. She'd gone right off the idea of ice cream. She just wanted Emily to get on with it.

'Ramona, Seaview House, where your gran is, is a nursing home especially for people who have something called dementia. Do you know what that is?'

'Yes, I do. And I know it's that sort of place because I looked it up. That's when I knew there'd been a mistake because Tilly hasn't got dementia.'

'That's just it,' Emily said. 'I'm afraid Tilly does have dementia, which has probably been coming on for some time.

That's why the hospital transferred her to Seaview House, so that she could be cared for by people who understand the illness.'

Ramona knew they were talking about Tilly, but it felt like they were talking about somebody else, a stranger.

'Which kind of dementia has she got?'

Emily's eyebrows went up a bit. 'She has vascular dementia. That's when...'

'I know,' Ramona said. 'It's when people have funny turns which are really strokes, only very tiny ones, and every time they have one it makes a little piece of their brain stop working. It's like losing a piece of a jigsaw. It leaves a hole.'

'You read about that, too? Ramona, you never cease to amaze me.'

'On the computer, yes. I didn't understand all of it, although I expect I would if I read it again. It is what I said, though, isn't it?'

'Yes, you described it very well. Do you remember Tilly being unwell recently? Did you see her fall down or anything like that?'

'No.' Ramona thought. 'I didn't see her. But there was one time, when I came home from school and she had a big bruise on her knee and a scrape on her elbow. She said she'd tripped over in the garden while she was hanging out the washing. Could that have been one of those little strokes, do you think? Is that why she fell over?'

'I don't know, love. I don't suppose we'll ever know. But the doctors carried out a lot of special tests at the hospital before they sent Tilly to Seaview House. They would have made sure that's what she had before they transferred her.'

Ramona leant closer to the table, closer to Emily. Her voice came out smaller than before.

'Can people with dementia forget all sorts of things, like,

where they are and where they live? Can they forget about people, even though they knew them very well before?'

Emily nodded and looked at Ramona, and Ramona looked at Emily and tried, very hard, not to cry.

Emily and Laura sat in garden chairs on the patio at Cloud Cottage and watched Ramona rolling a ball across the grass to Laura's granddaughter, Daisy, and encouraging her to roll it back. Daisy's mother, Holly, sat on a picnic rug nearby, her face turned up towards the sun.

It had been Laura's idea to bring her daughter and granddaughter to Emily's house for the afternoon. She thought that playing with the baby might help Ramona take her mind off Tilly for a while, and it seemed to be working. The girl seemed very taken with Daisy. Who wouldn't be? She was such a sweetie.

Emily had been telling Laura about the private fostering arrangement that had been put speedily into place, meaning that Ramona could stay with her, at least temporarily. Glenda Robertson had told her that Social Services were highly unlikely to move on that any time soon; there weren't enough real foster homes to go round, and children in far worse situations were given priority. Emily hadn't talked to Ramona about any of this – the child had more than enough to cope with already.

Since Emily had rescued her from Number One The Pasture, Ramona hadn't mentioned her fears about being put into a home or sent to live with strangers. Emily hoped that meant she'd put them out of her mind, although, knowing Ramona, it wasn't likely.

'How long do you plan to have her living here?' Laura asked, keeping her voice low.

'For as long as she needs to be here. As long as she *wants* to be here. As I said, nobody's going to be looking to place her elsewhere, not yet. They're exceedingly grateful I've taken her in because it gets them out of a spot. Glenda said that.'

'Yes, well, I don't wish to pour cold water on it, Em, and I won't ask if you've thought it through because I know you have, but...'

Emily laughed softly. 'I wouldn't say I've thought it through, exactly. I went with my instinct, and that was to do right by Ramona.'

'I was going to say, what about Ethan? He'll be back soon, won't he? How's he going to take having his passionate interludes curtailed by a twelve-year-old sleeping in the next room?'

Emily laughed out loud. Ramona, Holly and Daisy all looked across at her.

'Tell it like it is, why don't you?'

Laura giggled. 'Well, it's a fair point. You told me he didn't even like her being here for an hour or two after school. He's not going to be jumping for joy about all this, is he?'

'I know.' Emily sighed. 'We're already teetering on the edge as it is. At least I am... But what was I supposed to do? Leave her all alone in that cottage where goodness knows what might happen, or turn her over to Social Services and wave goodbye?'

Laura let a beat fall before she answered. 'Ethan's a grown-up, supposedly. He should understand you're doing it out of kindness and not to spite him.'

'Yes, well... But you know, if I'm honest, I'm not just doing this for Ramona. I really like having her around. She kept away from me for a while after school broke up, and I never did find out why. But she's back now, and that makes me happy. It's tragic about her grandmother, of course.'

'Yes, well, maybe you shouldn't get too fond of Ramona. Too attached.'

'I'm trying not to,' Emily said. 'It's not easy, though. She's such a character.'

'Yes, I got that.' Laura laughed. 'I heard her asking Holly earlier what it was like to give birth and whether Daisy came out head first or feet first.'

'She's not satisfied with generalisations. She likes the detail. Sometimes, she amazes me with her knowledge and her insight, and at other times she talks like a six-year-old.'

'I expect her upbringing's got something to do with it,' Laura said. 'Living in a cottage in a field with only her grandmother. It's not exactly conventional, or ideal.'

'Maybe not,' Emily said, 'but Matilda Donnelly's obviously done a good job. The girl's a credit to her.'

'Yes, that's true.' Laura nodded.

Their attention was drawn towards Ramona, who now had Daisy in her arms and was walking around the garden with her, pointing out the flowers.

'She's a natural,' Holly said. 'Daisy's very happy with all the attention.'

'So's Ramona, by the looks of it,' Emily said. 'She needed the distraction. She has another hurdle to face tomorrow and I haven't the foggiest idea how it's going to go.'

Laura frowned. 'What happens tomorrow?'

'I'm taking her to see Tilly.'

'I have been here before,' Ramona said in a matter-of-fact voice as she stepped confidently up to the front door of Seaview House. Emily reached above her and pressed the round brass button of the doorbell.

'Have you? When?'

'I brought a get-well card for Tilly and put it through the letterbox. My friend Lilah came with me. I didn't write my name in it, but I didn't need to because she'd have known it was from me.'

Emily had already heard Ramona's story about visiting Cliffhaven General and been impressed yet again by her bravery and resourcefulness. But coming to Seaview House was news to Emily. She wondered what else Ramona had done during these past weeks when she'd been on her own. Nothing would surprise her now.

'Ramona, Tilly might look a bit different from when you last saw her, and she may say things that don't make sense. It might be a bit upsetting for you, so you need to be prepared for that.'

'I expect she'll look pale from being ill and not being out in the sun, and be in a bit of a muddle. She'll still be Tilly, though.'

Ramona smiled brightly as if she was offering reassurance to Emily whereas it should be other way around. For a moment Emily felt slightly out of her depth. The girl's optimism was heart-breaking, but clearly that was how she'd coped since her grandmother was taken away from her. How she coped with everything life threw at her, probably.

Emily put a hand on Ramona's shoulder. 'You don't have to go in today, not if you don't feel ready. We can come back another time.'

But Ramona was already speaking to the uniformed young woman who had opened the door.

'We've come to visit Mrs Donnelly,' she said.

'You must be Ramona. I'm Karen. We've been expecting you. You're very welcome.' She smiled at Emily. 'Both of you.'

They were led through a lounge where other patients, mostly elderly, sat in semi-circle in front of a television, then out to a large, sunny conservatory at the back.

'I tried to sit Tilly on her own for her important visit,' Karen said quietly to Emily. 'It's worked so far.'

Several high-backed armchairs faced the garden. Only one

was occupied, by a woman with a neat appearance and youthful complexion, sitting perfectly still, her hands in her lap. Ramona rushed forward, then stopped dead and looked at Karen and Emily as if she needed permission to go up closer.

'Tilly, look, your granddaughter's come to see you,' Karen said gently. Then to Ramona, 'Go right ahead, lovely.'

Ramona stood in front of Tilly's chair, then ducked down to be closer to her height.

'Tilly, oh my Tilly! It's me. It's Ramona.'

The elderly woman stirred, her body giving a little twist as if she'd only just realised anyone was there, and then she smiled, a beautiful, warm smile. Emily saw echoes of Ramona.

'This is very nice.' Tilly reached out and patted Ramona's upper arm. 'Have you come to see me? Nobody said. Why didn't anyone say?' She glanced around, seeming confused.

'I've really missed you,' Ramona said. 'I waited and waited, and you didn't come home, but I've been all right, haven't I, Emily?' Emily nodded. 'So, you aren't to worry.'

Tilly made as if to get up out of the chair.

'Stay where you are, Tilly,' Karen said. 'I'll fetch some tea and cake, then you can have a tea party.'

'A party? Who's having a party? I'm not dressed! I can't go to a party in my nightie. Whatever will people think?' Tilly's eyes skittered about, her hands flapping against the chair arms.

'You haven't got your nightie on, silly,' Ramona said. 'You've got nice navy blue trousers and a pink jumper. And look, we brought clothes, some of your clothes from home. And some other things, just to last you while you're here.' She indicated the holdall by Emily's feet.

Karen and Emily exchanged smiles. Karen pulled two chairs forward for Emily and Ramona, then went off and a few minutes later returned with the tea on a tray.

'Her hands are shaky,' Ramona said, watching Tilly raise the cup slowly to her lips.

'Yes, but don't worry,' Karen said. 'It's normal. We offered her a cup with a lid and spout but she refused to use it.'

Ramona laughed. 'She would. Anyway, she doesn't need a special cup. Look, she's got the hang of it now.'

Emily turned and spoke quietly to Karen. 'Ramona is an eternal optimist. She understands how the dementia affects her grandmother, but I think in her heart of hearts she's still expecting her to get up out of that chair and come home, like nothing's happened.'

Karen watched Ramona helping Tilly to a slice of sponge cake. 'Take it a day at a time. That's all you can do. I'll leave you to it. I'll be back in a while.'

'This is a very good tea party,' Emily said, smiling at Tilly. 'Thank you.'

The old lady reared up, toppling sponge cake from her plate into her lap. 'What're you thanking me for? I didn't invite you!'

'Whoops, my mistake,' Emily said. Ramona giggled.

Tilly waved aside Ramona's efforts to clear up the cake and pointed a finger at her. 'You came to see me yesterday. And you were here in the night. I saw you!'

'I didn't come yesterday, or in the night. You're getting muddled. I'm Ramona. I live with you. Remember?'

'Ramona? No, no, that's not it! Who are you?'

Emily gave Ramona a warning glance: *Don't push it. Be patient.*

'She doesn't know me.' Ramona's eyes filled as she looked appealingly at Emily. 'My Tilly doesn't know who I am. She thinks I'm somebody else.'

'Darling, remember Tilly's very confused because her illness makes her like that. Deep down, she probably does know who you are, but she can't get at the memory. Don't be upset.'

Tilly suddenly lurched forwards as if she might topple right out of the chair. 'I know who you are now. Why didn't you say, you silly girl?'

Ramona's face lit up.

'You're Caroline! I said you'd come. I said all along, but they never listen. Nobody listens!'

'Oh,' Ramona bit her lip and looked at Emily.

'Well, she's nearly there,' she said. 'She knows you're family. She's one generation out, that's all. It's a start.'

'Yes,' Ramona said, seemingly placated. 'And I bet the next time I come she gets it right.'

'I would very much like a cheroot,' Tilly said. 'I hope you brought them.'

Tilly had fallen asleep in her chair, her head lolling to one side. Ramona asked to see where her bed was, and Karen took them upstairs to a bright, high-windowed room with a sea view. She shared the room with another female patient, which Ramona wasn't too happy about, but she was pleased about the view.

'I hoped she could see the sea,' she said. 'And now I know she can. I expect she likes that.'

Karen took the bag containing Tilly's clothes, retrieved earlier from the cottage, and stowed everything away in a locker, handing the empty bag back to Emily. Back downstairs, they found Tilly still fast asleep.

'Best not wake her,' Karen said. 'She can be confused if she's woken suddenly. More confused, that is...'

'Yes. I would like to go now,' Ramona said, and again Emily admired her bravery.

Ramona hardly spoke all the way home, and Emily left her to her thoughts.

'Do you think Tilly would like me to read to her?' Ramona said, as they arrived back at Cloud Cottage. 'I could get some books from the library.'

'You could certainly try reading to her. I think that's a great idea. Instead of taking books out of the library, though, how about bringing some of her own, her favourites? It might help trigger her memories of home.'

And of you, Emily thought, but didn't say it.

Ramona liked that idea. Emily promised they'd go back to Seaview House very soon.

As she unlocked the door of Cloud Cottage, she felt her phone vibrate in her bag. She put the kettle on before she looked at the message.

It was from Ethan. *Hello, you. Trust you're behaving yourself. Can't wait to misbehave with you when I get back. Love ya. Xxx*

She smiled and thumbed a reply. *Hello yourself. Right back at you. Love Em. xxx*

CHAPTER 23

The following day, Glenda Robertson came to Cloud Cottage. Ramona was called down from her room where she'd been arranging her collection of animal bones on the top of the chest of drawers – she'd brought them from home, along with her books and stuff, at the same time as they'd fetched Tilly's things.

The three of them sat in the living room, facing each other in an unnatural triangle. Ramona sat stiffly, feeling the tension in her neck and shoulders. She'd understood that certain things – formalities, Emily called them – had to happen if she was to be allowed stay at Cloud Cottage, but she had hoped that Emily would take care of all that and she wouldn't need to be involved

But it was okay, really. Glenda was kind and friendly. She had a round, pink face and a cushiony stomach. Her navy blue cardigan had a tiny hole in the elbow and her hair had gone a bit haywire as if she hadn't had a minute to drag a brush through it. These shortcomings made Ramona like her even more. All she said to Ramona was that she'd thought it was about time they met, and then she asked some questions about school and friends, and the things Ramona enjoyed doing. The questions were easy and after she'd answered them, Glenda smiled and thanked her, and said she could go back up to her room if she liked. She was about to say she'd rather stay, thank you very much, when Emily gave her a little nod, and she understood that staying wasn't an option.

Even so, after she'd left the room, she stayed by the closed door.

'She seems a well-balanced girl,' she heard Glenda say. 'Mature beyond her years, I'd say. But we have to remember she's still only twelve. If you have any worries at all, get in touch.'

'She's a joy,' Emily replied. 'It's a real pleasure having her to stay.'

They went on talking in lowered voices and Ramona had to strain to hear. She caught the words 'Tilly' and 'Seaview' and 'long-term care' and 'funding' and 'processes in this situation' but nothing else interesting. After a few minutes, she left her listening post, went back upstairs and carried on arranging the bones according to type and size, as they had been in her bedroom at home. When she was done, she picked up the sheep's jaw, complete with teeth, held it up in front of her, and made a face at it.

On Saturday morning, Emily drove Ramona to Lilah's house, even though Ramona had said she'd be totally fine going on the bus.

Emily had spoken to Sharon, Lilah's mum, on the phone the evening before. With Ramona's permission, Emily had told her everything that happened with Tilly, and about Ramona living alone in the cottage they shared; the whole story. They'd had quite a long conversation. Ramona had heard the sound of Emily's voice from upstairs but this time she'd resisted the temptation to eavesdrop.

She and Lilah spent the morning hanging out in the high street in Lilah's village, chatting and laughing all the time, which made everything feel much closer to normal, even though it actually wasn't, not really. So much was the same and yet, at the same time, so much had changed.

In the afternoon, Lilah's mum took the two of them to the cinema at Brighton Marina and McDonald's afterwards. Ramona understood perfectly why Emily had arranged a day out for her – it was to take her mind away from the visit to Seaview House when Tilly had muddled Ramona with Caroline, her mother. *As if she could ever forget.*

But she wasn't too upset about that, not now. She'd read enough about dementia to realise it wasn't the real Tilly who'd got into a muddle. It was just Tilly's brain telling her those things because it had gone all funny and stopped working properly. But the doctors would soon fix that – yes, she knew what she'd read, and what Emily had told her, but they didn't know Tilly like she did. Neither did they know Ramona, not properly. She and her gran were a team – Tilly had always said that. Together, there was no problem they couldn't solve. It was just a matter of time.

Ramona and Lilah had already arranged to see one another today anyway, although she'd let Emily believe it was her idea. When Emily had dropped her off at Lilah's house, Ramona thought to ask how she planned to spend her day, and how she hoped she'd be doing something nice.

Emily had smiled and said 'bless you', as if someone had sneezed. She could be dead old-fashioned for a fairly young person, Ramona thought. Then she'd said she was going to the newspaper office at Cliffhaven, then returning to Cloud Cottage to do some work. It didn't sound very exciting. Ramona thought about Ethan. He'd be having a much better time up in Yorkshire, she was sure. It didn't seem fair. Texting Emily every five minutes hardly made up for it, did it? Emily hadn't said anything about the messages that kept pinging through, but it was obvious they were from Ethan by the way Emily smiled as she read them, turning her phone slightly away from Ramona in a secretive sort of way.

She wondered what would happen when Ethan came back. She wasn't looking forward to that, and she didn't imagine he'd be exactly over the moon to find her staying at Cloud Cottage either. He had recognised her at the school opening evening, as much as she'd recognised him; she could tell by the way he'd looked at her before he'd rushed off with his family – if that was who they were. He must be wondering all the time whether she'd said anything to Emily. Ramona was convinced now that there was no innocent explanation for Ethan's sudden appearance at her school – how could there be?

And so, the problem remained. Should she let Emily carry on believing that Ethan was a decent boyfriend and was being faithful to her, or should she confess to her friend what she'd seen and let her decide what to do about it? Lilah said that in a case like this the woman had a right to know, but she'd been talking hypothetically. It wasn't so simple when it was happening right in front of you. Not simple at all.

She would keep quiet, for now. She felt a bit mean, and cowardly, but it didn't feel like the right time to go upsetting the apple cart, as dear Tilly would say. She would just stay watchful, and wait and see.

As promised, Emily took Ramona to Seaview House again. They went twice more, with Emily coming in to see Tilly the first time, and the second time, she went off and did some shopping while Ramona went in on her own.

The reading had so far been a great success. She'd chosen a

couple of Agatha Christies, a 'Miss Read' book, and a handful of the historical romances Tilly favoured. They'd sat in the conservatory again, and Tilly had shown definite signs of recognition when Ramona showed her the book covers. She'd smiled and nodded, and her eyes had livened up. She didn't seem up to choosing one, so Ramona had chosen for her – one of the Agatha Christies that had a boathouse on the cover.

It wasn't a very long book, which was one reason Ramona had chosen it. It was hard to tell whether Tilly was listening at first. Her watery eyes had half-closed, and she hadn't looked very 'with it' at all at one point. But as soon as Ramona stopped reading, Tilly's eyes had opened fully.

'Well, carry on, then,' she'd said, in exactly the same voice she always used when she was telling Ramona off in a jokey way.

The familiarity of it, this glimpse of her Tilly, had felt like sliding into a warm bed on a cold night.

After the first two visits, Ramona persuaded Emily she could make the journey to the nursing home on her own. She tried not to mind Emily forgetting she'd be thirteen in a couple of months and had been travelling around on her own for totally *years*. She probably couldn't help being overprotective. It wasn't Emily's fault she'd been landed with a girl she hardly knew, was it? Ramona thought about how she'd tagged onto Emily over the library fine and felt guilty about it, but only a tiny bit.

'I know, I know, you're not a baby,' Emily had said. And then she'd apologised and explained how she felt extra-responsible for her because of the 'situation'.

That word was getting a lot of use lately. Ramona wasn't sure she liked being a *situation,* but she couldn't think of a better word either.

Emily rang Glenda Robertson, the social worker.

'I don't think Ramona's accepted that her grandmother isn't coming home soon. She's got a good grasp of what vascular dementia is and what it does, but it's as if it's all theory and doesn't apply to Tilly.'

'She's young, she's been through so much these past weeks. I suspect she's in denial, and her head tells her the reality, but her heart says there'll be a magic cure and it will all be fine,' Glenda said. 'Do you want me to have a word with her?'

'No, I don't think so, thanks. I just thought I should mention it. I think it's probably best to let her work it out for herself. I don't want her to come crashing down when she does get it, though.' Emily sighed into the phone.

'Emily, I can't emphasise enough how grateful I am – *we* are – that you've taken Ramona into your home. At some point we'll be looking for long-term foster care for her, but there won't be any movement on that for a while. Meanwhile, you're doing fine, believe me.'

Emily let a beat of silence fall, before she said, 'Glenda, this is purely theoretical, but if Ramona does need a foster parent, what would be the chances of me being considered?'

'Excellent, I'd say. But remember, it's one thing having her to stay on a temporary basis and quite another taking her on full-time.'

'I know. As I say, it's only theoretical.'

One afternoon, Ramona came bouncing into Cloud Cottage after a visit to Seaview House, calling out Emily's name.

'In here!' She closed the laptop as Ramona landed in the living room with a thud.

'Guess what? Tilly remembers home! I was reading to her and suddenly she said she needed to water the raspberries and the beans, and then she said about the plums having to be picked before they went rotten! We have got raspberries and beans, and a little plum tree. She remembers her garden! Isn't that wonderful?'

Emily smiled. 'It is. You must be so pleased.'

'I am, and do you know what? Karen said it's probably the reading. Apparently, being read-to can bring back parts of the person that have been lost, and it doesn't just trigger memories, it can help them think for themselves again. They've done a study of it at a university – Liverpool, I think. If I read to Tilly enough, then all of her might come back, mightn't it?'

There was such excitement and hope in Ramona's eyes. Emily had to fight the urge to hug her. She'd almost attempted it several times, but the message in the girl's body language was clear. She didn't want that sort of closeness, which showed how vulnerable she really was.

'Ramona, don't get your hopes up too much, will you?' Emily said gently. 'Go on with the reading by all means because you gran obviously enjoys it, but she has been quite poorly in herself. It's not just about memory.'

'I know.' Ramona looked resigned rather than disappointed. 'I could look it up on the internet, though. There's bound to be lots more about it.'

'Yes, I'm sure there is.'

Emily wasn't sure whether delving deeper into the clinical reports on Tilly's condition would help, or whether she'd end up getting really confused and not liking what she was reading. But the girl had a natural thirst for knowledge on all kinds of subjects, and Emily couldn't have stopped her if she'd tried.

'So, is it okay if I pop home and get her some more books tomorrow?' Ramona asked, still bright and full of optimism.

'Ramona, you don't need to check in with me when you want to call in at Number One. It's your home. If you ever want a lift, though, you only have to ask.'

'Yes, thank you, Emily.'

Ethan sent another text – not one of his sweet, sexy texts, but one carrying a much more important message.

Emily had been sitting in the car in the car park of the *Cliffhaven News*, waiting for the sudden downpour to stop, when she'd texted him on impulse.

Can't wait to see you next week! Time's going too slowly. Em xxx

Usually he didn't reply straight away so when the return 'ping' came moments later, it took her by surprise, but not as much as the message itself did:

Change of plan. One of my mates is heading up to Edinburgh. Asked if I wanted to go. Seems too good a chance to miss. Hope you don't mind. Love you. xxx

Well, yes, she did mind. She minded one hell of a lot. Several questions arose at once: He told her he loved her, virtually every day, so why wasn't he rushing back to see her? Did he take her so much for granted that he thought it was fine to keep her waiting like a spare part and turn up when he felt like it? And when, exactly, *did* he plan on coming home?

She dismissed them all as pathetically needy. Instead, she texted back: *Great. I've been to Edinburgh and you'll love it. Send me a postcard. Xx*

/ CHAPTER 24

f she couldn't be at home, Cloud Cottage was the next best place to be, Ramona thought. Emily was so lovely, arranging her work and reporting assignments so that she didn't have to leave Ramona on her own for long stretches at a time, even though she'd be fine, and had said so.

If Emily had been out and Ramona knew she was on her way home, she would have the kettle on and the mugs out, with the biscuits, ready for when she came in. Apart from dusting her bedroom, helping with the washing and things, and running to the village shop, there wasn't much else she could do to make up for Emily being the totally coolest adult in the world, apart from Tilly. Maybe one day she'd find a way.

She was such a regular visitor to Seaview House now that all the staff knew her and made time to chat, especially Karen and Saleema, who mostly cared for Tilly between them. Ramona tried not to mind the old people who shuffled about, looking plain awful, and those who suddenly shouted out for no reason. It wasn't their fault, was it? She hoped Tilly didn't mind them too much, although she didn't seem to notice.

The reading was going really well. Tilly had begun to take an interest in what Ramona read to her now, and she made sure she had a good selection of books with her, as well as the parish magazine that came through the letterbox once a fortnight, and a copy of the *Cliffhaven News*, provided by Emily.

It was funny how life turned everything around, Ramona thought, remembering how Tilly used to read to her, not only at bedtime but at other times too, especially in winter when it was too cold to go out. They'd snuggle up together in Tilly's chair with the fire leaping and dancing in the grate, and Tilly would read her favourite stories to her, as many times as she liked. And now it was her turn to read to her grandmother.

One afternoon, she was reading out an article from the *Cliffhaven News* about restoring an old water tower in a field somewhere when Tilly's eyelids began to droop and it looked as if she was falling asleep. Then, as Ramona was about to put the paper aside, she suddenly sat bolt upright, grabbed the paper from Ramona's hand, and flung it onto the floor.

'That's not news! They've been going on about that since Lord Lucan went missing!'

Ramona burst out laughing, although she had no idea who Lord Lucan was. The corners of Tilly's eyes had crinkled up, as if her eyes were laughing while the rest of her face couldn't quite make it.

'Not that one, then.' Retrieving the paper from the floor and putting it back together, Ramona opened it a different page and there was the piece Emily had written about the proposed library closures. 'Okay, this is a bit more interesting.'

She showed Tilly the photo of the outside of Charnley Acre library that went with the article. It didn't seem to register with her, but she sat very still and listened, really listened, while Ramona began to read article and the comments alongside it.

Before she got to the end, Tilly interrupted.

'Books! The books have got to go back! Is the library open

today? I've been here for *two* days. Have I missed the library? What day is it today, Ramona?'

Ramona stared at Tilly, watching her plucking at the material of her skirt in her agitation about the library books. It didn't matter – she'd calm down in a while. Nothing else in the whole world mattered now, because Tilly remembered her.

'Tilly, oh my Tilly,' Ramona said through her tears. 'You *do* know who I am, don't you? Say it again, Tilly. I'm Ramona. You say it.'

But Tilly just looked at her, long and hard, and then she reached out and touched the ends of Ramona's hair with a look of wonder on her face.

'Brown hair. Lovely shiny brown hair, like a bird's wing,' Tilly said, so softly that the words hardly made a sound.

But Ramona heard. 'Yes, I've got brown hair, the same as yours used to be.'

'Where's Caroline? Is she coming? Tell her I've been waiting for her.'

'No, she's not coming, Tilly. Caroline was my mother. She was my mum, but she died, a long time ago.'

Tilly's eyes filled with sadness. Ramona jumped up and wrapped her arms around her, so tightly she could feel the bird-like flutter of her heart. When Tilly wriggled, she let her go, sat down again and took Tilly's hand in hers, rubbing gently. The skin felt warm, dry, familiar.

'Who are you, then?' Tilly said after a while.

'I'm Ramona, remember?'

'Ramona! Yes, that's it! How good of you to come and see me.'

Tilly's face broke into a wide smile.

CHAPTER 25

It seemed as if a miracle had taken place at Seaview House, Emily thought. Ramona certainly thought so. Now that Tilly had recognised her and called her by her name, she was transformed. She'd seemed contented before – happy, almost, in her own quiet way – but now she raced in and out of Cloud Cottage, visiting her grandmother, seeing Lilah and her other friends, and always with a smile and a light in her eyes that, Emily realised, had been missing before.

Emily crossed her fingers metaphorically and hoped for the best.

Then, one afternoon, she'd stayed at the office until almost six to write up a report on a cliff fall which had happened that morning, a little way along the coast. The traffic on the Cliffhaven road had slowed her journey, and she hadn't arrived home until almost seven.

Something was different; she sensed it as soon as she walked in. The cottage seemed uncommonly quiet. Ramona always let her know if she was going somewhere, or she'd been at Lilah's and was late getting home. Emily had texted her own estimated time of arrival and got no reply, but she'd thought nothing of it.

She went upstairs, calling Ramona's name. Perhaps she was in her room with her headphones on. Emily opened the door. The room was empty. Items of clothing were strewn on the bed – a pair of black leggings, a grey jersey dress, a pink t-shirt – as if they'd been discarded or forgotten. One of the drawers in the chest was pulled out and Emily could tell some of the items were missing. The dressing table top had been cleared, and Ramona's rucksack, the one she used for school, was gone, too.

On her way back downstairs, her heart racing, Emily rang Ramona's mobile. It went straight to voicemail. In the living room, Emily's laptop stood on the table, its lid open. She sat down in front of it, heeling her hands against her eyes for a moment before she moved the cursor and woke up the screen. The blackness cleared, revealing the site she'd been looking at last night: *Fostering Legislation in England.* The tabs for other sites, including government sites about children left with no parent or guardian, were open at the top of the screen. Information, that was all she'd wanted. She'd sat down last night with a glass of wine and browsed, out of interest, and curiosity. And because she cared about Ramona's future, whether it involved her or not.

There was no point in alarming Lilah's parents – Sharon would have phoned or messaged her if Ramona had turned up there. And she knew full well what the outcome would be if she tried Ramona's mobile again.

Moments later, stopping only to shut down the laptop, Emily jumped in the car and drove to the only place Ramona could be: Number One The Pasture.

She parked on the road outside, not on the property itself. Instinct told her not to call out and make a fuss. She stood to one side, where the trees and bushes shielded her from the house. The Downs were painted with purple shadow, and gossamer strings of pink and apricot threaded the deepening blue sky, but the house itself stood in full light, the late sun glancing off the windows like lasers. Moving from her hiding place, Emily went quickly to the front door and knocked, experiencing a flash of déjà vu from the last time she'd come here to seek out Ramona.

Nobody came. She wasn't surprised. Ramona had obviously run away; she was hardly likely to give herself up that easily. Emily walked carefully around the outside of the house. She looked at the windows, but the curtains were all drawn tightly so she couldn't see inside. She felt justified in calling out now. She was responsible for the girl; she couldn't leave her here.

'Ramona! Please come out. Come out and talk to me. Please?'

Nothing. Emily called again, this time through the letterbox.

'Ramona, you know you can't stay here. Please don't make this harder than it needs to be. Come on, lovey. You're not in trouble. It's only me, Emily.'

And then, when there was still no response, she put her mouth to the letterbox again: 'I'll stay here all night if I have to.'

She'd sounded sharper than she'd intended but her anger was building now, anger directed at herself rather than Ramona. This was her fault. If she hadn't been so lazy last night, she'd have shut down the laptop properly. But she'd been tired and it was late, so she'd gone straight up. Ramona was free to use Emily's laptop whenever she wanted to – it was faster than her own. Emily should have thought about that and been more careful.

She'd tried so hard to make Ramona's life at Cloud Cottage seem as normal as possible. Helping her young charge to live in the present and be reasonably happy had seemed the best thing she could do for her. There was plenty of time to face the future when they had to.

And now it looked as if she'd gone and ruined it all by one

careless moment. There could be no other reason for Ramona's flight.

Emily walked round to the back of the house, clanging her foot against a metal watering can which stood by the tap. Ramona must have heard it and known where she was. But all that mattered was finding Ramona and taking her back to the safety of Cloud Cottage.

With little hope of luck, Emily levered the handle on the back door. It opened. She went inside and called again. No response. She made a tour of the cottage, downstairs, then up. All the doors were open, all the rooms empty. Ramona's room had a desolate air about it, many of her possessions having gone with her to Cloud Cottage. Only the bed showed signs of recent occupation – the pillows were banked in a haphazard heap against the headboard, the duvet was rumpled and dented.

Feeling the tug of anxiety in her gut, Emily went back downstairs, had a last look round, and left by the back door. If Ramona wanted to play games, fine. She could just get on with it.

You don't mean that, said Emily's inner voice. Of course, she didn't. But if Ramona wouldn't co-operate and let Emily try and sort this out, what on earth was she supposed to do? Not the police, not yet. But she could ring Glenda. If she was off duty, she'd send somebody. There must be emergency cover. The word 'emergency' sent cold shivers down Emily's spine. She stood at the corner of the property, where the garden melded into the bushes, watching the house for any signs of movement, anything at all.

And then, something made her look across the field. At the furthest corner stood a broken-down wooden hut. Emily picked her way across the rutted grass. The hut had no door but stood in a finger of shadow from the hills. It took a while to focus her eyes as she peered inside. Ramona was sitting on the floor in the corner, hugging her drawn-up knees, a bulging rucksack by her side. Her eyes shone a challenge in the half-dark.

Emily didn't speak. She just held out her arms.

'No,' Ramona said, pushing herself tighter into the corner. '*No.*'

'Darling, I think I know what this is about. I can explain and we can talk about it, but first let's get you home.'

'I *am* home. This is where I live.' Ramona spoke calmly, but with a slight quiver in her voice.

'Yes, I know. I meant *my* home, which is yours, too, for as long as you need it.'

Ramona unfurled herself and sprang to her feet. Scooping up the rucksack, she pushed past Emily, rushed out of the hut, and set off across the field. Emily followed, feeling worse than useless. As she watched Ramona's back view, her determined stride, the proud squaring of her shoulders, she wondered how she'd ever imagined she could foster a twelve-year-old girl, especially a complicated one like Ramona. She had no experience; she wasn't up to the task. That was the bald truth.

But that didn't alter the fact that she had to deal with this situation, and it had to have an acceptable outcome for Ramona.

She'd stopped in front of the cottage. Emily, lagging behind in her backless sandals, had visions of Ramona slamming indoors and locking herself in before Emily could reach her. Seemingly not. She whirled round as Emily approached.

'I trusted you, and now you're going to send me to one of those places where kids go who've got nobody else. You *promised,* but you're a liar! I don't need you. Tilly said my name. I'm getting my Tilly back and I don't need you! Leave me alone!'

'Oh God, Ramona, it's not like that. I wanted some information because I care about you, that was all. Nobody's sending you anywhere, until—'

'Until! You said until! See, you were lying!'

Emily stood facing Ramona. She felt at a complete loss. All she'd done, or tried to do, was take care of Ramona until the situation with her grandmother was resolved, in whatever way. But it was clear now that Matilda Donnelly wasn't coming home, and Ramona, whatever she pretended, must realise that.

This sweet, quirky, intelligent girl was scared out of her wits.

Emily swallowed and kept her voice level. 'Okay, I know you think I'm the Devil Incarnate and I can live with that. But the fact remains that you can't stay here on your own. It isn't safe, and it isn't legal. And right now, I'm your only option, so it looks like you don't have a choice, wouldn't you say?'

Ramona shrugged, letting her rucksack drop to the ground. 'I thought you'd be pleased to have me out of the way when...'

'When what?'

Ramona lifted her chin. 'When Ethan comes home. You won't want me hanging around then, will you? He definitely won't. He hates me, and I hate him.'

'*Ethan*? Ramona, he's got nothing to do with this. Cloud Cottage is my home. Ethan doesn't get to choose who I invite. Why do you hate him, anyway? Why do you think he hates you? You've only met him once, maybe twice.'

Ramona shook her head slowly, her gaze meeting Emily's. Emily had no idea what was going on, but she had the distinctly odd feeling that Ramona had the upper hand.

'I wasn't going to tell you,' she said. 'I couldn't stand you not knowing, but I didn't want you to be upset either, and if you had it would have been all my fault.'

'Well, whatever it is, I think you'd better tell me, don't you?'

'What, now?'

'Yes, now. Please.'

Ramona gave a big sigh. The fire seemed to have gone out of her. She'd had enough; she was ready to give in. 'Okay.'

The story came out, piece by piece, of what had happened at

the school open evening. Not that there were many pieces to it. It was all very simple, in the end. Ethan had been caught playing happy families with a woman who was not Emily and a child she knew nothing about. The oldest story in the world.

'Sorry, Emily,' Ramona said, when she'd finished.

'No need. You were right to tell me.' Emily found a smile. 'Shall we go now?'

Ramona nodded. 'I just need to lock the back door.'

Emily almost followed her in case she locked herself inside the house, but it was all right – she was back in less than a minute.

They drove to Cloud Cottage in easy silence, the sweet scents of a summer's evening drifting in through the car windows.

CHAPTER 26

The following morning, Emily rang Laura.

'I'm going stalking. Want to come?'

'Ooh, yes please! Sounds intriguing.'

'It's all you're getting, for now, anyway. Are you in?'

'I'm in. Whatever it's about. I could do with a bit of excitement.'

On her way to Spindlewood to pick up Laura, Emily dropped Ramona off at Holly and Isaac's house in the village. She'd been there before to play with Daisy, and loved it. Emily had quietly rung Holly this morning and, without giving much detail, asked if Ramona could spend a couple of hours with them today. Holly was sensible; she knew to contact Emily if she was worried.

Emily and Ramona had had a heart-to-heart last night, and Ramona had seemed much calmer about everything. Emily had been honest and said she didn't know what would happen in the future, but for now Ramona should think of Cloud Cottage as her home – her second home – and she was to talk to Emily if she was worried about anything at all.

'I'm sorry I ran off,' Ramona said. 'I got scared when I saw all the stuff about homes for kids like me. I know I'll have to live somewhere eventually, until I'm an adult. Just not anywhere horrible, with awful people.'

'Nobody is going to send you anywhere horrible,' Emily had said. 'And that is something I *can* promise, because I would never let that happen.'

It wasn't an answer, not really, because there wasn't one, and Ramona knew it.

She was quiet for a while, thoughtfully drinking her hot chocolate in bed while Emily sat on the side.

'I didn't mean to upset you about Ethan,' she said, after a while. 'I think I must have wanted to punish you when I... But that was wrong, and I'm sorry.'

'Don't be,' Emily had said. 'You shouldn't have to carry around a secret like that. It's too much.'

'What are you going to do?'

'I shall have to think about that, very carefully.' Emily had smiled in a conspiratorial way and tapped the side of her nose.

Ramona had tilted her head to one side. 'This love business isn't as easy as you'd think, is it?'

She'd sounded so serious that Emily couldn't help giggling, which made Ramona giggle, too.

'I think I know what we're doing here,' Laura said, as the car swooped under the tunnel from the seafront road and into Brighton Marina. 'This is Ethan's territory.'

'Yep.' Emily still hadn't told Laura about what Ramona had seen, or anything more about why they were here. She needed to keep her own perspective and not confuse her thinking with anyone else's, although she had a fair idea as to what Laura's take on it would be. Laura, typically, hadn't asked questions. She was just being the supportive friend she always was. 'I haven't planned this at all but I have to do something, that's all I know. I shall play it by ear.'

They parked in the multi-storey and walked along the boardwalk, past the bobbing boats and the restaurants, to the residential part of the marina where Ethan worked and lived. The blocks of apartments had wide windows and attractive fern-green balconies, most of which contained patio chairs and tables, ready for the residents to sit and look out over the sea.

Ethan's apartment was on the sixth floor of the second block along – the top floor, because he needed good light for his graphic design work.

'Have you got a key?' Laura asked, as they approached the side entrance with its double row of intercom door bells. Some of the bells had discreet name-plates by the side.

'No, never had one. This is probably a wild goose chase but I just want to check something out. Call it gut instinct.' With no real expectation of a response, she pushed the bell beside the plate which said *Ethan Pateman Designs*. After a moment, a male voice spoke huskily via the intercom: 'Yes, can I help?'

'That's not him, is it?' Laura hissed.

'No. It must be one of his design team.' Laura put her mouth closer to the intercom and summoned her best business voice.

'Hello, I'm Isabella Winters and I'm here about a logo design.'

'Isabella Winters?' Laura giggled, and found Emily's hand across her mouth.

'You'd better come up then,' said the disembodied voice. The buzzer went.

'I'd better do this on my own,' Emily said. 'It'll seem more authentic.'

'Okay, I'll go and grab a coffee.' Laura looked slightly disappointed. 'Text me if he holds you hostage.'

'Yes, very funny.'

The man who let her in was tall and good-looking, with shoulder-length dark blonde hair, swept back. He introduced himself as Alex – Emily had heard Ethan mention the name. She allowed herself to be shown through to the studio as if she'd never been here before.

'Can I get you a coffee, Isabella?' Alex asked, already on his way to the kettle. 'I was just about to make one.'

'Yes, I'd love one. Thanks.' She seemed to be talking through her nose, as if she wanted to disguise her voice, though there was no need.

'Milk? Sugar?'

'Just milk, thanks.'

'Won't take a sec. Have a seat.'

Emily looked around while Alex had his back to her. The studio was familiar, with its set-up of drawing boards and computer screens, and walls papered with design samples. The rooms along the corridor she knew well, too, of course. The bathroom on the left, the small bedroom next to it, the large living room on the right, overlooking the sea, and next to that, sharing the sea view, the master bedroom.

Next to her chair was a pin-board. Emily scrutinised the contents. Meaningless notes, company fliers and business cards were pinned at random. One of the cards, she noticed, was for Ethan's own business. She'd seen his old business card ages ago – in fact, there was one pinned up in the office at work. This one was new – an eye-catching, temporary design, cream with stylish burgundy lettering. On impulse, she whipped the card from beneath its pin and slipped it into her bag, just as Alex turned and came back with two mugs of coffee.

'Now,' he said, sitting down on the opposite chair. 'You said something about a logo. For your business, is it?'

'Yes, but I've already discussed some initial ideas with Mr Pateman – Ethan – and I can see he's not here. I was in the area, so I thought I'd call in and share a couple more thoughts I've had, but I'll get in touch with him another time.'

'What kind of business is it?'

'A café, in a village high street. Charnley Acre, just north of Cliffhaven.'

Immediately the words left her lips, she regretted them. Too much information, too much detail. She'd trip herself up if she wasn't careful.

'Charnley Acre? Heard of it but can't say I know it.'

'It's a very small place.' Emily smiled. 'How do you like working here? At the marina, I mean? It's a great outlook from up here.'

The question sounded inane to her own ears but she'd thought it prudent to steer the conversation into neutral territory, away from further mention of Ethan. A little small-talk wouldn't go amiss. After all, she was drinking his coffee.

But Alex didn't bite. Clearly, small-talk wasn't his thing.

'It's fine. Mostly I don't notice what's going on outside. Have you brought anything with you, your design ideas, on paper? I could take a look if you like.'

'Ah, no, I haven't brought anything. As I said, I was in the vicinity so...' Emily put her half-empty coffee mug down on the desk. 'I'm sorry, I'm taking up your time. I remember now Ethan saying he was going on holiday.' She stood up. 'Thanks for the coffee.'

'You're very welcome.' Alex smiled, and widened his eyes, just perceptibly. 'Ethan will be sorry he missed you, Isabella. I'll tell him you stopped by when he gets back from Cornwall.'

'Cornwall? I thought he said he was going to Yorkshire. I must have mixed him up with someone else.'

'Nope, it was definitely Cornwall. They've got a holiday home somewhere near Padstow. All right for some. Mind you, you wouldn't get me down there in August. Too crowded and nowhere to park. If you're stuck with the school holidays, though, what can you do?'

Emily experienced a curious sense of freedom as she made a rapid, adrenaline-fuelled exit, using the stairs instead of the lift, and almost cannoning into Laura who was waiting at the bottom.

'How d'it go?'

Emily raised her eyes. 'Tell you in a minute.'

It was twelve o'clock; Laura had already had coffee so they found a table outside one of the boardwalk restaurants and ordered salads, bread, and white wine.

Emily downed half of her small glass of wine in one go.

'I know I'm driving, but I need this. The bread will soak it up.'

'It better,' Laura said. Then, 'So...?'

Once Emily had regaled Laura with the history to this expedition, as well as what had just taken place, her friend's reaction was predictably succinct.

'Bastard!'

'The trouble with me,' Emily said, 'is that I don't concentrate. I use up all my concentration in one go when I'm working, and that's it. I don't see the signs.'

'Or you do, and you choose to ignore them.'

'Yep.'

Emily fished in her bag, pulled out Ethan's new business card, and put it on the table. 'I pinched this. I don't know why.' She ripped it in half and dropped it onto the table with her screwed-up napkin. 'Hang on...'

'What?' Laura peered at the half of card in Emily's hand. She'd turned it over to look on the back.

'This mobile number's not the one in my phone. It's not the one he's been texting me from for the last three weeks.'

'It'll be his work mobile, then, won't it?'

'He doesn't have a work mobile. He uses the same one for everything.' Emily had her own mobile in her hand, scrolling to Ethan's name.

'Emily, have you heard him talking to business clients, or anyone else, on his mobile while he's with you?'

'No. He either takes it outside if he's on a call or switches it off so we won't be disturbed. It's one of the things I like about him. *Liked.*'

'Well, maybe now he does have a separate phone for the business.'

The two women looked at each other.

'Only one way to find out,' Emily said.

She switched her phone to speaker and tapped out the number on the card. The call was picked up at once. A sweet-toned female voice skipped across the table.

'Hi, this is Helen, answering Ethan's phone. He's in the pool right now. Who is that?'

'Sorry, wrong number,' Emily trilled, matching Helen's cheeriness.

Cutting the call, she put her phone down and looked at Laura.

'He's got a separate mobile all right, only it's not for work. It's for me.'

CHAPTER 27

At breakfast one morning, Emily suddenly said to Ramona, 'I think we deserve a treat, the two of us, don't you?'

Ramona wasn't sure she deserved anything after the way she'd behaved, running away like a five-year-old so that poor Emily had to chase after her and fetch her back. And then, to put the tin hat on it – as Tilly would say – she'd blurted out the story of Ethan turning up at the school open evening without stopping to think how it would make Emily feel.

It was true what she'd told Emily – at that moment, she'd wanted to get back at her because she thought she was about to be packed off to a kids' home. It had been a knee-jerk reaction after she'd seen that stuff on Emily's laptop. Only she'd got it wrong. She wasn't stupid – she knew she couldn't stay at Cloud Cottage forever – but right now, she didn't have to go anywhere else. She should have known Emily wouldn't let her down. She'd been so kind, giving her a home when she needed one, and Ramona had virtually thrown it back in her face.

So, no, she didn't deserve a treat, and said so. Emily didn't agree.

'Nonsense. Ramona, you're a marvel the way you've coped with everything. I could never have been so strong at your age – at *any* age – so you'd better believe it.'

A marvel. The word made Ramona think of Spiderman and Captain America. Kids' cartoons. She'd never much liked animated films. It was while her mind was veering off down this track that Emily asked if there was anything special she'd like to do for her treat. When Ramona hesitated, Emily came up with a list of suggestions, counting them off on her fingers.

'Theme park, zoo, castle, boat trip, the i360 on Brighton seafront... better than that, the London Eye!'

Ramona thought. 'It's your treat, too. What would *you* like to do?'

'Me?' Emily smiled. 'As long as you enjoy it, that will be my treat.'

Ramona didn't think that was very fair on Emily, but she'd obliged and given it some thought. Finally, she'd come up with the barbecue idea.

'I could invite some of my friends and you could invite some of yours, and then it would be fun for you as well. I'd help with the food so you didn't have to do it all.'

'A barbecue? Are you sure you wouldn't rather go out somewhere for the day?'

Another time, perhaps, she would like that, but right now, doing something special right here at Cloud Cottage, where she felt safe, would be perfect.

Emily understood right away, she could tell. 'Right, pass me the pad and pen and we'll make a list of scrumptious food and drink,' she said.

'Can we have marshmallows?'

'Of course. I'll put them as number one.'

The barbecue took place on Saturday afternoon. Lilah came, with her mum and her little sister, Sophie. Mila, Aysha and

Freya from school came, too. Emily's guests were Laura and Clayton, Holly and Isaac, and baby Daisy. Emily's friends were Ramona's friends now. Knowing that gave her a warm feeling inside. Looking around the garden at everybody made Ramona felt as if she was part of one big family, and her heart performed a little skip.

The only person missing was Tilly. Ramona flipped burgers on the big gas barbecue, borrowed from Laura and Clayton, and willed herself not to be sad, not today.

Ramona's mind was still on the barbecue and what a fab time they'd had, and how everyone had stayed for absolutely hours until it was almost dark, when Emily drove her to Number One The Pasture on Sunday morning.

She'd planned to walk, but as she was leaving, the sky suddenly darkened to a purplish grey and thunder growled in the distance. Ramona wasn't afraid of storms – she and Tilly used to love watching the lightning from her bedroom window – but Emily was right, there wasn't any point in risking a soaking.

Ramona plumped down in Tilly's chair next to the cold, ash-filled fireplace. She should clean it out, some time. Definitely before Tilly came home.

'Wasn't it brilliant yesterday, at the barbecue?' she said, for at least the fifth time today.

'It was.' Emily sat down on the sofa. 'I'm glad you enjoyed it. I certainly did.'

'Did you miss Ethan, though?'

It might have been the wrong thing to say, but the question just popped out.

Emily smiled, and shook her head.

'No. Well, maybe just a tiddly bit but that was only out of habit, and Ethan is one habit I can kick into touch, no problem.'

'Oh. Well, that's good then.' She paused. '*Is* it good, Emily?'

'Absolutely. If it hadn't been for you, I might have gone on seeing what I wanted to see and been blind to everything else.'

'I think you would have seen the other things, eventually. If you'd wanted to.'

'Mm, are you sure about that?' Emily gave a little laugh.

Ramona shrugged. 'I don't know. I don't know a lot of things, really. I expect I will in time, though.'

This was starting to feel a little bit awkward, as if she was out of her depth, and she half wished she hadn't asked the question. She supposed she'd wanted to check in with Emily in case she was really unhappy about Ethan. But, unless she was hiding her feelings well, she seemed fine. She also made it seem normal to discuss her love life with a twelve-year-old, so that Ramona didn't feel she was poking her nose into something that was none of her business.

Emily leaned forward on the sofa. 'Ramona, if ever you want to ask me anything, about the facts of life and growing up and all that kind of stuff, go for it.'

Even more awkward!

'It's cool,' she said airily. 'Tilly told me all about it ages ago, and we did it at school, so I think I'm all right for now, thank you.'

Emily seemed to be holding in a smile. At the same time, she looked relieved as well as a tiny bit embarrassed.

'Ah, yes, of course. At your age you would know all about it.' Emily stood up. 'Right then, go and fetch whatever it is you need, and we'll get home before the rain, with any luck.'

'Tilly's bed socks,' Ramona said. 'She told me her feet get cold in the night. I don't know if she meant it or if she'll remember saying it, but I thought I'd take them, just in case.'

As she was passing the phone, she noticed the winking light.

'Oh, look, there's a message. Two messages.' She pressed the play button.

Message 1. Tilly, are you there? It's Mary. I'm home now and can't wait to see you. Give me a buzz, darling.

Message 2. It's me again. Where are you, and where's Ramona? I've been ringing and ringing, and I came over yesterday and all locked up. Where the devil are you?

Ramona put a hand to her mouth. She'd forgotten all about Mary, with everything else that had been going on.

'Who's Mary?' Emily was by her side now, gazing at the answer machine.

'Tilly's best friend. We had a postcard from her when she was in Canada.' She fetched the card from the kitchen windowsill and handed it to Emily.

Emily studied it for a moment. 'Okay. This we need to do something about. Would you like me to get in touch with her, or would you rather do it?'

'You, please.'

Ramona couldn't imagine putting into words everything that had happened. If Mary got upset about Tilly, she wouldn't know what to say.

'Leave it with me.' Emily noted the number from the answer machine, jotted it on the postcard, and slipped it into her bag.

On Monday afternoon, Emily finished work early and arrived home at three. She'd warned Ramona to be ready, and they drove straight down to Seaview House. It had been raining hard all day and the wind was churning the miserable grey sea into massive waves which roared and crashed onto the pebbly beach.

Ramona and Emily clung to one another's arms as they made their way to the door, laughing as they struggled to stay upright in the gale. Saleema stopped them as they signed the visitors' book, then headed for the conservatory where Tilly sat in the afternoons.

'She's not too bright today so we kept her in bed. We think she might have had another little TIA in the night. Go on up. She's in a smaller room now, right next to the other one. The door's open. I'll pop up shortly. She's already got a visitor, by the way.'

The other visitor was Mary, Ramona knew. She felt a wobble in her stomach, firstly because Tilly wasn't where she usually was, and secondly because Mary might be cross with her for not getting in touch sooner. She'd have to explain that she didn't have Mary's phone number, and even if she had, she didn't know she was back from Canada.

She needn't have worried – not about Mary, anyway. She was sitting on the side of Tilly's bed, not in the chair. When she saw Ramona, she gave her a wide smile and stretched out an arm towards her.

'It was quite a shock, hearing about your gran. I had to come and see for myself.' She stood up and put her hands on Ramona's shoulders. 'And you, young lady, I hear you've been up to all sorts! What a girl!'

'Not all sorts,' Ramona said, frowning.

'Just joking.' Mary's eyes darted across her face. 'You look fit and healthy anyway. One out of two's not bad, I suppose.'

She winked and Ramona grinned. She knew how much Mary cared about Tilly, and the joking was for Ramona's benefit. She'd forgotten how much she liked Mary.

She remembered her manners. 'This is Emily. Emily, this is Mary.'

Ramona left Mary and Emily to chat at the end of the bed. She went to Tilly and kissed her cheek. It felt hot. Hotter than usual.

'Aren't you very well today? Poor Tilly.'

'There's nothing wrong with me that a couple of tablets and a bit of fresh air won't sort out. Honestly, they make such a fuss!'

Ramona's heart soared at this snapshot of the real Tilly. But it sank again when Tilly coughed, and went on coughing, making horrible grating sounds in her chest.

'That nice nurse said she's got a chest infection on top of everything else,' Mary said. 'She had one before – of course, you'd know about that. Apparently, the doctor's put her on a course of antibiotics.'

Mary sank into the chair by Tilly's bed and gave a little sigh. 'She's too young for all this. She might be eighty-one but that's no age these days.'

Wasn't it? Eighty-anything seemed positively ancient to Ramona. She was brought up short by this sudden reminder of Tilly's age. It wasn't something she thought about usually, and Tilly certainly never mentioned it.

'I know. It's a devil, this condition. It's not confined to the elderly, either,' Emily said.

'It's called vascular dementia,' Ramona said, moving proprietorially as close to Tilly as she could get without actually getting into bed with her.

She saw Emily and Mary exchange a smile. Well, you had to give things their proper names. Tilly believed in plain speaking and so did she.

Tilly raised herself from the banked up pillows and took hold of the sleeve of Ramona's cardigan. 'Who are you, then?'

'I'm Ramona. Remember?'

'Ramona,' Tilly said, stretching the name out. She smiled. 'If you say so, dear.'

Ramona stayed with Tilly for longer than she usually did. For some reason, Emily and Mary went off together to talk, presumably about Tilly, although what on earth there was to talk about she had no idea. Surely it was the doctors' job to sort out her gran, and they just had to wait to be told what they were doing for her.

But she liked being left alone with Tilly. The new room was quiet and peaceful, with nobody else sharing it. It had more stuff near the bed than before: a cylinder thing, machines with buttons, and leads running around. It all looked very complicated. Ramona tried not to think about it. She was pleased the room still had a view of the sea so there was something interesting for Tilly to look at while she was stuck in bed.

She had brought some books with her, as usual. Tilly didn't seem interested, but she sat in the chair and read a few pages to her anyway. Her voice sounded different in the quiet room, too loud and kind of echoey, in a way that it never did in the conservatory. After a while, one of the care assistants, a man, brought tea and sponge cake for Tilly. The tea came in a sippy cup with a lid on it. Ramona waited for Tilly to complain, but she didn't. She didn't drink more than a few sips of the tea. She didn't touch the cake.

Ramona put the books back in the bag. She rearranged Tilly's pillows and helped her to sit up a little more, then found her brush in the cabinet and gently brushed her hair for her; it had got awfully untidy because she'd been in bed all day.

After a while, Mary came to say goodbye to Tilly while Emily waited for Ramona downstairs.

'I'll come and see you tomorrow, love,' Mary said in a cheery voice, as she kissed Tilly on the cheek. 'You have a nice rest now.'

But Tilly just looked at Mary through sleepy eyes and said nothing.

'Come on, lovey,' Mary said, holding out a hand to Ramona. 'Time to go home.'

'In a minute,' Ramona said. 'You go down and I'll follow you.'

Alone again with her grandmother, Ramona levered herself up onto the bed.

'You just make sure you get better quickly, my Tilly. And then we can read some more books together. We could even go for a walk and look at the sea. You'd like that, wouldn't you? I brought your bed socks – they're on top of the cabinet. Get the nurse to put them on for you, then you won't have chilly feet in the night.'

Tilly stared as if she was looking right through Ramona and out the other side. It made the tears gather, but Ramona wouldn't let them fall, not in front of her grandmother. She had to stay strong. Except it wasn't easy to do that, not any more.

And then Tilly lifted her head from the pillow. Her face came alive again and her eyes danced as they darted across Ramona's face.

'Caroline! They tried to keep you away, but I knew you'd come. It is you, isn't it?'

'Yes.' Ramona smiled. 'It's me, Caroline.'

'What were you talking to Mary about?' Ramona asked, as Emily drove them back to Charnley Acre. 'Was it about Tilly, or me?'

'Both, in a way,' Emily said. 'Have you heard of something called Power of Attorney? Lasting Power of Attorney, in this case.'

Ramona thought. 'I've heard the words, but I don't know what they mean.'

Emily explained. It appeared that Tilly had arranged for Mary to have this attorney thing – she'd done it ages ago –

which meant that she would take over Tilly's money and act on her behalf for all the important things, if ever she couldn't do it for herself and Ramona was too young.

'It's good news,' Emily said. 'It will help everything along, you'll see. Mary's great, isn't she?'

'Yes, I really like her. I've known her all my life, practically.'

Ramona fell silent. Emily glanced sideways at her. 'Okay?'

'Yes. Tilly won't ever be able to do those things for herself now, will she?'

'No, darling, she won't. I'm sorry.'

'It's fine,' Ramona said, staring straight ahead, through the swishing windscreen wipers.

But of course, it wasn't fine; they both knew that.

It was five o'clock the following morning when Ramona, not quite asleep but not quite awake either, heard movement from Emily's bedroom across the landing. She thought she'd heard the beep of a phone, and then Emily's voice, low and indistinct.

In seconds, she was out of bed and running to Emily's room. 'It's Tilly, isn't it.'

She didn't really need to ask. She just knew.

Emily nodded, and sat down on the unmade bed, the phone still in her hand. She patted the bed and Ramona sat down next to her.

'Tilly had a stroke about an hour ago, a big one. They've taken her to hospital. Ramona, I'm so sorry.'

'Is my Tilly going to die?'

'We hope not, but it's possible. We'll just have to wait and see.'

Ramona got up off the bed, went back to her own room, and closed the door behind her. Emily didn't try to stop her. She stood by the window, watching the sky through the trees as it slowly turned from denim blue to pink to a light grey-blue. A new day. Everything different. Everything changed, again.

After a while, she went back to Emily's room.

'Can I see her?'

'You could. Nobody's going to stop you, but the hospital doesn't advise it, not at the moment. Tilly's in intensive care. She isn't conscious. She won't know you're there.'

Ramona thought for a moment, then she nodded. 'I don't think I want to see her like that. She would understand, wouldn't she, if she could?'

'Definitely. Mary knows – I rang her earlier. She'll keep in touch with the hospital and let us know what's happening. Shall we have an early breakfast? The birds are having theirs, by the sound of it.'

Emily's window was open, and the birds were chirruping away outside.

'Shall I have my shower and get dressed first?'

She felt five years old again, a little girl, wanting to be told what to do.

'If you want to. Otherwise, come down in your pyjamas. That's what I'm doing.'

Emily stood up and slid her feet into flip-flops. They went downstairs together, Ramona in her new pyjamas, the pretty blue ones Emily had bought her as a present. Her feet were bare. Surprisingly, she felt quite hungry and managed a bowl of cereal and a piece of toast.

'Is there anything particular you'd like to do today?' Emily said, when they'd finished breakfast.

'Just stay here, please. I might read my archaeology book.'

'Okay. I'll be here, too,' Emily said, her voice all light and casual. 'I don't have to go anywhere today.'

'Thank you,' Ramona said, and went upstairs to have her shower.

*E*mily had talked to both Mary and Glenda on the phone while Ramona was out of earshot. Mary and Glenda had spoken to each other, and to everyone else involved in an official capacity. Ramona's future was assured, her long-term future as well as her immediate one. She didn't know that yet. The time would come when the details would be explained to her; she had enough on her mind for now.

Ramona hadn't left Cloud Cottage for two days, except to run down to the village shop and back in double-quick time, even though she'd made Emily promise to ring her mobile the minute there was any news and not wait until she was back. But if she felt easier staying at home, that was fine. Emily made sure she was around, too. She worked on a couple of articles, conducted two interviews on Facetime and kept in touch with her editor, and otherwise kept an eye on Ramona while she – while they both – stayed on full alert for the phone. Mary reported back on Tilly twice a day, by text to Emily. Not that there was much to report; her condition hadn't changed.

On Saturday, the weather turned from wet and windy to

gloriously hot and sunny. Lilah phoned and asked Ramona if she wanted to go to the beach at Cliffhaven. Emily was pleased when she agreed to go. A change of scene and the company of her friend could only be good for her. She seemed calm and content as she set off for the bus stop, a picnic lunch in her rucksack.

Emily was even more pleased that Ramona was out when there was a knock on the front door and she opened it to find Ethan standing there. Either he knew she'd rung his mobile – his real one – or Alex had mentioned her visit to the marina office. Possibly both. Okay, she'd given Alex a false name but if he'd described her and her implausible reason for turning up on spec, he'd have worked it out. The fact that he hadn't walked straight in through the back door as usual and the carefully orchestrated contrite expression on his face meant he definitely knew something was wrong.

'Emily.' He sounded breathless, as if he'd been running, although his car was parked in front of the house.

But as much as she needed to talk to Ethan and bring this latest chapter in her woeful love life to a close, it was suddenly all too much. Her focus was firstly on Ramona, and, almost equally, on her work. Combined, those things were enough.

'I can't do this now,' she said.

'Please, Em. I need to explain.'

Sighing, she held the door open for him. 'You haven't got long. I have to go out on an assignment.'

If that wasn't true before, it was now. There'd been another cliff fall in almost the same place as last time. One of the freelance reporters had covered it yesterday but the professionals would be attending the site today, including a geology professor from the university, and the editor wanted an in depth piece about the erosion of the cliffs in East Sussex.

She could have gone to the site tomorrow and talked to the

geology professor on the phone, but actually, now that Ethan had turned up, having somewhere else to be was a relief.

She led him through to the living room but didn't ask him to sit down. He sat down on the sofa anyway, looking far more comfortable than he had any right to, under the circumstances. Emily sat on the chair farthest away from him, folded her arms and waited.

'Em, I'm so sorry for letting you think I was in Yorkshire when I wasn't.'

Ah. Alex, then.

'And Scotland.' She wasn't going to let him forget the second lie.

Ethan dropped his gaze to the carpet. He looked suitably apologetic but it was all an act, wasn't it?

'You were in Cornwall, I believe.' It wasn't a question.

'Yes, I was, but...'

No, he wasn't going to wriggle out of this by feeding her another fairy story.

'You're married, aren't you? To Helen.'

His head flicked up. 'How do you know about Helen?'

Okay, so he hadn't been told about her 'wrong number' phone call. *Good.* He hadn't been prepared for that. It gave her an advantage.

'Never mind how I know. It's true, isn't it?'

'No. Helen and I were together for seven years, but we never married. It wasn't what either of us wanted at the time. I have... we have a daughter, Saffron. She's almost ten. Helen and I split up two years ago, although I was still a father to Saffron and saw her as often as I could. Then, six months ago, Helen said she wanted to give it another go. We'd been to a wedding together because Saffron was a bridesmaid, and it was easy, you know? We talked a lot and got on well. Helen took it into her head that our differences had resolved themselves. I wasn't so sure, but we started seeing more of each other and things kind of moved on from there.'

'When you say 'moved on' what does that mean?' She flapped a hand. 'Oh, don't bother explaining. I know exactly what it means. I'm not stupid.'

Ethan said nothing. She was trying to remain calm, she really was, but her anger was already threatening to boil over. He didn't look in the slightest bit embarrassed or ashamed. It was then that she fully understood how she and Ethan might have been close in other ways, but emotionally? Not a chance.

'Right, so you were sleeping with your ex when we met. For God's sake, Ethan! After all the things you said to me, and how we were together... What a fool I've been!' She threw up her hands. 'Okay, no. I wasn't a fool, because you're the coolest of liars and a damn fine actor. How the hell you kept it up for so long, I'll never know. No doubt you would have gone on living your disgusting double life if you hadn't been found out.' She wasn't going to bring Ramona into this. If he had any decency, he wouldn't either.

'Emily, don't, please.' He looked as if he was about to get up and come to her, then thought better of it. 'It wasn't quite the way it sounds. The timing was way off, I admit...'

'You *admit*? That's rich...'

'I know, and I was going to sort it all out. I know you won't believe me, but it's true.'

'So, what were you going to do, then? Does she, *Helen*, know about me? No, of course she doesn't! That's not the way you operate it is? Telling the truth.'

'Emily, please. Let me explain properly.'

'Oh, I think you've explained very well already.'

He shook his head, quite violently. 'No, listen, it's not that simple. This is hard for me, too.'

'Oh, well, I'm sorry about that!'

'*Please*, Em.'

She met his gaze; the new softness in his eyes almost floored her. She loved this man. *Had* loved him. The romantic, warm-hearted part of her still did. Now that he was here, in the same room, it wasn't so easy to rip that feeling into shreds and throw it out with the rest of the rubbish.

And so she sat, and she listened, and what she heard was, in a way, worse than the clichéd scenario of a family man having a girlfriend on the side. She could have understood that whilst obviously not condoning it.

Ethan had been seeing his ex at the same time as he'd been going out with her, and sleeping with both of them. He confirmed that now; he couldn't very well not. During that time he'd been quietly weighing up his options. His ex-partner, the mother of his child; or Emily? The extended sojourn at the Cornish holiday home was supposed to be the ultimate test. Whether Helen looked at it in the same way, he didn't say, and Emily didn't want to know. She'd already heard as much about Helen as her emotions could handle. But as far as Ethan was concerned, the holiday had been make or break time.

'I'm not in love with her, Em, I know that now. She's not in love with me either, although she says she is. We had problems right from the start of our relationship, if I'm honest. And then we had Saffron and that brought us closer for a while, but it didn't last. We both knew we were over long before we admitted it and I moved out. If I'd stayed, we would have ended up killing each other. Then, when she wanted me back, the physical side confused me at the time, but that's all it was. And that's gone now, too. I don't... I don't want Helen in that way, and I'm not in love with her. But I *am* in love with you. And that's why I've told her it's over for good, and why I'm moving out of the home we shared, again.'

His eyes appealed to her; his whole demeanour appealed to her. But Emily was focussed on one thing only.

'You're moving *out*?'

'Yes, tonight, as it happens.'

'Out of where, exactly?' Her question sliced through the space between them like cold, serrated steel.

'Our house. Mine and Helen's. I moved back in a while back.'

'A fact you conveniently forgot to mention five minutes ago.'

'Yes, sorry. But I'm telling you now.'

'I can't believe this.' Emily spoke in a whisper, to herself as much as to Ethan. Her hands gripped the arms of the chair. 'Where is this house?'

'Just east of Cliffhaven.'

'*Cliffhaven*? You've been living practically on my doorstep the whole time? My God, Ethan, no wonder you were able to pop in and out of here so easily.'

Ethan ignored this and carried on.

'As soon as I moved back into the house, I regretted it. But we were both working, so it wasn't as if we were together twenty-four-seven, and it made looking after Saffron easier. I didn't lie to you about that, Em, not really. I do stay in the apartment at the marina overnight sometimes, for convenience. I suppose you could call it a *pied-a-terre*.'

'Hah! A little convenience by the name of Emily!'

Ethan raked his fingers through his hair, making it stand up in peaks. 'It was never like that. You were – are – a big part of my life.'

'So big a part that I had to be hidden away, never going out anywhere local where we might actually be seen, and whisked back to Cloud Cottage or to your shoebox of an apartment under cover of darkness. Very nice, I'm sure. Very chivalrous.'

A look of exasperation passed across Ethan's face. His eyes widened, a faint red blush showed on his cheeks. It was, she realised, a familiar look of his when things were not going his way. But in terms of his inner feelings, it meant nothing.

'We're wandering off the point here. Emily…'

'No.' She stood up and moved round to the back of her chair. 'If you're about to declare your undying love for me, then save your breath.' Ethan opened his mouth, but she held up a hand. 'You turn up here, knowing you'd been found out for being a two-timing pathetic loser, then insult me by telling me I'm the chosen one, and expect me to fall gratefully into your arms. Well, it's not happening. Not now, not ever. And I'd like you to leave now, please. As I said, I have somewhere else to be and time's getting on.'

She went to the door of the living room. Ethan got up off the sofa but remained standing in the middle of the room.

'Emily, I know you've got feelings for me. You can't switch them off just like that…'

'Oh, believe me, I can, and I have.' It wasn't one hundred percent the truth, but inching nearer all the time. 'In any case, I've got much more important things to think about. I'm looking after Ramona at the moment while her grandmother's in hospital. A grandmother who, for your information, is probably dying as we speak.'

Ethan had the grace to look shocked. Whether that was because she'd mentioned Ramona or because of the situation with Tilly, she couldn't tell, but she'd place her bets on the first option.

Ethan's hands hung loosely by his sides. The contrite look was back.

'I'm sorry to hear that. And I'm so sorry, Emily, for the way I've behaved. It was unforgiveable, I know that, but maybe in time…'

'Ethan, please go now, and don't contact me again.'

A pause, then he nodded sharply and walked past her out of

the room, to the front door, his mouth set in a grim line. As he passed her, she caught a breath of the expensive *eau de toilette* she'd bought him for his birthday. What did he do, scrub it off before he went home to Helen, or pretend he'd bought it for himself? The diversion of the farcical scenario helped her mind stay in focus as, without warning, Ethan leaned towards her in the doorway, kissed her on the cheek and whispered, 'I love you, Em. I always will.'

'Goodbye, Ethan,' she said, and closed the door after him.

Ten minutes later, Emily jumped in the car, fully intending to go to the cliff fall site. But as she reached the crossroads, impulse took over and, ignoring the Cliffhaven fork, she drove up Charnley Hill to Spindlewood.

Laura opened the door with a broad smile.

'This is a nice surprise. Clayton's down at Holly and Isaac's house, helping to take down some old apple trees in their garden. I was about to do some prep for the new term, but you've saved me just in time.'

'I'm playing truant, too. I should be standing on a cliff top now, talking to a geologist about coastal erosion.'

'And the fact that you're not,' Laura said, leading the way along the hall to the kitchen, 'must mean something's happened.'

'I never said that.'

'You didn't need to. Oh, it's not Mrs Donnelly, is it?'

'No, nothing's changed there. We're still waiting on that one.'

'So, if it's not Ramona's gran, my money's on Ethan.'

'Yep, that's the one.'

Laura rubbed her hands together. 'Right. What do you want to do? We could have coffee in the garden, or go out somewhere? Your call, Em.'

'That's the trouble. I don't know what I want to do.' She gave a hollow laugh. 'God, I sound so pathetic!'

'No, you don't. Look, I'll stick the kettle on and we can just sit right here, and you can tell me all about it. Or not. No talking necessary.'

'It's tempting, but I don't think that'd work just now.' There needed to be something to go alongside the inevitable talking, something active. If she just sat, she might very well crumble, like the cliff. 'How about I go back to Plan A and you come along for the ride?'

The summer Saturday traffic slowed the journey and it took over half an hour to reach the site of the latest cliff fall. By the time they'd arrived, Laura had heard the full story, starting with Ramona's encounter with Ethan at the school open evening. She was speechless with outrage on Emily's behalf.

Well, not quite speechless.

'What an arse! I had my doubts about him, you know that, but only because he wasn't giving you the attention you deserved. What d'you think he'll do? Go crawling back to Helen and tell her she's the one he wants after all?'

'I really have no idea, and I don't care. He won't be setting his size nines inside Cloud Cottage again, that's for certain. If he does show up, he's even more of a loser than I thought.'

Emily drove onto the parking area near the top of the cliff, where several vehicles already stood, including a police car, a Land Rover, and a minibus with the university's logo. An oblique view of the cliff face showed jagged edges like broken teeth, and below, a perfect pyramid of pure white chalk hugged the undercliff path and spilled over onto the beach. A long section of the beach and the steep steps leading down to it were cordoned off with red and white tape.

A number of people stood about on the section of the cliff top that was outside the cordons. Some, like the police officers, were obviously there in an official capacity, notebooks and clipboards in hand, serious cameras slung round necks; others were interested bystanders. A drone cruised overhead, like a giant wasp. There wasn't just one geologist but a whole crew of them. Emily went up to the eldest, guessing correctly that he was the professor she'd made contact with, shook his hand and gave him her business card.

'My students,' he said, indicating the group around him. 'They're a dedicated lot, seeing as it's a Saturday and out of term-time.' He gave a little laugh and his eyes sparkled with humour. 'Shall we go over there and talk?'

Emily looked over at Laura, gave her the thumbs up, and followed the professor to a quieter spot a little further along the swathe of grass. The students stayed behind, taking photos of the erosion on their mobile phones.

Twenty minutes later, Emily returned to Laura, who'd sat down on the springy turf.

'Did you get what needed?' She shaded her eyes to look up at Emily.

'Yes, he was really helpful. I can ring him next week if I need to check anything.'

'He seems young to be a professor,' Laura observed, widening her eyes meaningfully. 'Nice hair.'

Emily laughed. 'You can stop that right now. The last thing I need is another bloke, and that's my final word.'

'Seriously, though,' Laura said, as they drove back along the coast road. 'Have you had any thoughts about the future? About what you might do?'

'Do?' Emily smiled. 'I don't need to do anything except

carry on as before. Only now I'm free, and right at this moment that's as good as it gets. Of course, I've got Ramona to think about.'

Laura let a beat of silence fall before she broached the subject of Emily's fostering idea.

Emily sighed. 'It was a daft idea. Thank goodness I didn't say anything to Ramona. I'm not what she needs. She needs a proper family set-up. Tilly obviously did a wonderful job of bringing her up single-handed, and Ramona's completely devoted to her. But now, whatever happens with Tilly, she needs more than I could give her.'

Laura nodded, understanding. 'I wouldn't put it quite like that. She's clearly very fond of you, and the two of you would have worked it out between you, no problem. But I think you've made the right decision.'

Even if she had wanted to foster Ramona, Emily thought, she'd have stepped down. There were others, one person in particular, whose wishes in respect of Ramona's future rightly took precedence. But she couldn't say so to Laura. Not before Ramona herself knew.

'I might, when it's all over, go and work somewhere else,' Emily said, changing the subject as she manoeuvred the car around a stationary bus on the Cliffhaven road. 'I could try London again.'

'Oh, you mean get a job on a newspaper, or a magazine, like before?' Before her divorce, Laura meant. 'That was a manic existence, though. You said so at the time. And all that travelling, the trains and the Tube!'

'I could rent a little place in London and come back to Sussex at weekends.'

Laura looked sideways at Emily. 'It sounds as if you've thought about this before. Before today, I mean.'

'I've toyed with the idea, yes. There's nothing to stop me now.

It needn't be London. I could go to New York, or anywhere. The world doesn't begin and end at Charnley Acre.'

Emily smiled into the mirror. Laura returned the smile, a little sadly.

'You'll always come back, though.'

'Oh yes. I'll always come back to Cloud Cottage. It's my haven, the place I've been happiest.'

CHAPTER 29

The angels came for Tilly this morning, as dawn slipped into day. Tilly had never believed in angels. Ramona wasn't sure she did either. But perhaps they could both make an exception, just this once.

Emily hugged her when she broke the news – the first time she'd done that; Ramona hadn't minded at all. They they'd a little cry together. Ramona sat on her bed in Cloud Cottage for most of the day, not crying, just talking to Tilly inside her head. And remembering. Emily popped her head round the door a few times to ask if there was anything she could get her – there wasn't – but otherwise left her alone.

In the days that followed, the sun still shone, and the flowers still bloomed and dropped their petals, and the rabbits still ran across the fields, and the birds still sang, and the people still walked up and down the high street, and the clock on St Luke's Church still chimed the hour.

And all, strangely, without Tilly.

Ramona had once told Emily about a secret lane where blackberries grew in abundance; secret to her and Tilly, and now to Emily, too. They took an old basket from under the stairs in Cloud Cottage, went to the secret lane, and filled half the basket with ripe fruit. When they got home, they used some apples they already had and made a blackberry-and-apple pie together.

'It has to be pie, with proper pastry. Not crumble. Tilly couldn't stand crumble.'

More days passed. People came, phones rang, arrangements were made.

Ramona wore her smartest dress and said goodbye to Tilly. Only in public, though. She would never say goodbye in her heart.

A week later, Mary came to Cloud Cottage.

'Ramona, there are certain things that Tilly wanted you to know, concerning what happens now, and in the future.'

'What happens to me, you mean?'

Ramona looked at Emily, and Emily gave her a little nod and a smile, as if to let her know everything was fine.

'Yes. If there's anything you don't like or understand, we'll talk about it together.'

'What are the things she wanted me to know?'

'I think,' Mary said, looking at Emily, 'the best person to tell you is Tilly herself.' She handed Ramona a pale blue envelope with her name written on the front in Tilly's loopy handwriting. 'She wrote you this letter last year and gave it to me for safekeeping.'

Ramona looked at the envelope for a long time. Then she said, 'Is it all right if I take it home and read it?'

'Of course,' Emily said. 'Would you like me to drive you? I could wait outside.'

'No, I'll be fine to walk.' She turned to Mary. 'Thank you for bringing my letter. I expect I'll see you soon.'

When Ramona arrived at Number One The Pasture, she didn't go inside the house. Instead, she walked across the field, past the hut, and let herself out through the gate at the top. Beyond the gate was a narrow path, no more than a track, littered with rabbit droppings and flattened by passing feet, which wound its way up the slope of the Downs. She climbed up a little way, sat down in the long grass, and opened the envelope. Inside were several sheets of Tilly's best blue notepaper, covered in her writing. Ramona took them out and began to read.

My dearest Ramona,

As you are reading this, I expect you're feeling a little bit sad, and I'm so sorry about that, my darling. Wherever I am now, I want you to know I love you very much, and it's been my pleasure and privilege to have brought you up. In spite of that, you've turned out to be the loveliest, most wonderful girl! I am the luckiest grandma!

Now, to get down to practical matters. If you are still a child (in the eyes of the law), you'll need somebody to take care of you, and in my opinion, and I hope in yours too, the best person for the job is our friend, Mary. I don't know if you knew this, but Mary and her husband are what they call registered foster carers. That's why there were always children around in their house for you to play with. Mary couldn't have children of her own but, boy, has she made up for it!

So, Ramona, that is the first thing. If you are in agreement, you will go to live with Mary and she will take care of you for as long as you need. It might feel strange at first, suddenly being part of a big family, but that's all right. I'm sure once you get used to it, you'll be happy there and have a lot of fun. Mary is very fond of you, almost as much as I am!

The second thing is money. You are not to worry about that side of things because it's all taken care of. I haven't left you a fortune, I wish

I had one to leave! But with what I've put by over the years, there'll be enough to see you through.

You may already know this by the time you read this letter, but Mary is also handling the financial side of things and she will explain it all, in time. She will also tell you that I put an extra sum aside for your university education. If you choose not to go to university when the time comes, that's perfectly all right, my love. Use the money for anything you like, no strings. But you're a bright girl, and I know you'll work hard at school, and there's no reason why you shouldn't become an archaeologist, and a very good one, too. Or you can be anything you like – the world is yours, and you should follow your dreams. Always remember that.

Now, the house. I've left Number One to you, and everything in it, of course. The house has to be held in trust until you are eighteen, which is when you can legally be the owner. Sell it, keep it, rent it out, do anything you like with it. It will be your extra bit of security.

Well, my love, I think that's about it. Now, you go and be happy, and have a wonderful life. I'm sorry your life with me has been a bit on the quiet side, but we've had fun, haven't we? Remember those times, and try not to be sad.

Bless you, darling. All my love forever and a day,
Tilly x

She read the letter twice, then carefully folded it and put it back in the envelope. She sat for a while, hugging her knees and thinking, and looking down at the little house through misted eyes.

And when she'd thought enough, she held her hand over the place where her heart was, and where Tilly now was, too. Then she got up and walked down to the gate, across the field, and all the way back to Cloud Cottage.

CHAPTER 30

$\mathcal{M}$ary thought it would be best if Ramona was settled into her new home before school started again. Emily thought so, too. But there was no rush, they both said, and nobody was going to make her do anything she didn't want to do.

Which really meant she should get on and do it.

And so, Ramona moved out of Cloud Cottage and into Mary and Richard's big, modern house on the edge of Lewes, taking with her Emily's promise that they'd still be friends, and knowing she'd be welcome at Cloud Cottage any time.

Her new bedroom looked out over the back garden, and the back gardens of a lot of other houses. But at least she could still see the Downs in the distance, which reminded her of Number One The Pasture – not in a sad way, but in a peaceful, remembering kind of way, which was fine. She shared the bedroom with a dark-haired girl called Alice, but it was a big room and the beds weren't too close together. Close enough to have a chat and a giggle at night, though. Alice was a year younger than Ramona, but they got on really well right from the start. She was starting at Ramona's school, so they'd be able to go on the bus together, Mary said.

There were two other foster-children in the house: Philip, who was eleven – Ramona remembered him from her visits with Tilly – and an eight-year-old called Paul. Sometimes Ramona had to put her headphones on to block out the racket they made, even if she wasn't playing music, and then Mary would clap her hands and bellow *'Quiet!'* Not that it made any difference. Mary had a very loud voice for such a small person.

Ramona didn't have to wait long to see Emily again. There was a party at Spindlewood, Laura and Clayton's house, and Ramona and Lilah were invited. Ramona asked Emily what the party was for, and Emily said it wasn't for anything in particular. Laura just felt like having one, which sounded a good enough reason to Ramona.

The house was so big it was made for parties, she thought. It was cosy and homely, too, though, and the little circular room inside the turret was amazing. It had its own staircase leading off the upstairs landing. Laura took Ramona and Lilah up there to see it, and left them there on their own, for as long as they wanted. They imagined they were princesses locked in a tower, and then laughed at themselves for being so childish. But childish was just what you needed, sometimes.

Emily brought a man to the party with her; a quite good-looking man, who was a professor of geology. Laura seemed to find this funny for some reason. She and Emily got very giggly at one point. That could have been the fizzy wine they were knocking back, of course. The professor was very interested in Ramona's collection of animal bones and asked her to explain where and how she found them, which was nice. He told her about the pieces falling off the cliffs, which, as it turned out, was a lot more interesting than you'd have thought.

'You should go and have a look some time,' he said. 'Emily will take you.'

Emily had come up to them and said, 'What will Emily do?'

When Ramona told her, she said what a good idea, and the professor went all twinkly-eyed as he looked at her.

Ramona waylaid Laura in the hallway.

'Is the geology professor Emily's new boyfriend?'

'Not quite, but watch this space.' Laura tapped the side of her nose, and she and Ramona had a good old giggle.

Later on, Laura's husband, Clayton, came over to Ramona at the buffet table.

'How would it be,' he said, 'if I popped over to your house and gave the garden a sort out? I expect it's getting overgrown by now. Only if you'd like me to, of course. It's absolutely your shout.'

'*My* house?' He meant Number One – she hadn't twigged that for a moment. 'Oh yes, it has got rather out of hand. That would great, if you've got the time.'

Clayton had smiled, a big beaming smile that he quickly pulled back into an ordinary one.

'It would be my pleasure, Miss Donnelly.'

And so, it was arranged that Clayton would call in at Number One The Pasture whenever he had a spare hour, and keep the garden under control. The garden had been on Ramona's mind a bit; she would never be able to cope with it all on her own. But now the problem had been solved.

People were lovely, in the main, weren't they? There was kindness all around; that was one thing Ramona had learned these past months. You just had to look properly to find it.

The autumn term had begun and they'd been back at school for two weeks when Lilah nudged Ramona in the ribs as they sat in the canteen one lunchtime.

'See that boy over there, the one with the dark hair swept back? No! Don't look now!'

'Too late,' Ramona said. 'He's seen us looking.'

'Oh, God.' Lilah put her head in her hands, ever the drama queen.

Ramona turned her attention back to her cauliflower cheese. 'What about him?'

'Don't you think he's utterly gorgeous? *And*, he sits next to me in art. *And*, we had to share a box of pastels last week because there weren't enough to go round, and his hand kept touching mine.'

Ramona smiled and raised her eyes. Some things never changed. And the things that did, well, you just had to get on with it. That's what Tilly would have said.

She looked at Lilah. 'Let's hope I don't have to thump this one for you.'

'What d'you mean?'

'Oh, never mind.'

ACKNOWLEDGEMENTS

As always, my grateful thanks go to the brilliant team at Bloodhound for all the hard work that has gone into the making of *A Welcome at Cloud Cottage*. It looks amazing, so thank you all.

This is the third book set in the fictional village of Charnley Acre, and I hope I've managed to capture some of the charm of a typical Sussex village as the stories go along. Finding homes for my characters is so often a case of observation rather than imagination. I was on the top of the South Downs, at Devil's Dyke, when I looked down and spotted a little white cottage all alone in the corner of a field. It just had to be Number One The Pasture, Ramona and Tilly's home. So, thank you to my husband, and resident chauffeur, Michael for driving me around the county and not complaining too much when I've suddenly asked him to stop while I snap a cottage or gate that I just know belongs in my village!

Again, as always, my heartfelt thanks go to my lovely readers. I hope you've reading enjoyed *A Welcome at Cloud Cottage* as much as I did writing it. Thank you all so much.

A NOTE FROM THE PUBLISHER

Thank you for reading this book. If you enjoyed it please do consider leaving a review on Amazon to help others find it too.

We hate typos. All of our books have been rigorously edited and proofread, but sometimes mistakes do slip through. If you have spotted a typo, please do let us know and we can get it amended within hours.

info@bloodhoundbooks.com

www.ingramcontent.com/pod-product-compliance
Lightning Source LLC
Chambersburg PA
CBHW050615190726
48283CB00007B/2429